Vilma,

Thanks for you support! Enjoy.

Best,
Nicole

Father, Can You Hear Me?

A Novel

By Nicole Scott

Father, Can You Hear Me?

Written by Nicole Scott

Published by Pa-Pro-Vi Publishing

www.paprovipublishing.com

ISBN: 978-1-7374348-9-4

Printed in the United States of America

DEDICATION

For Mom and Dad

Part One

All That Glitters Ain't Gold

1

August 1991

"Baby, I don't understand why we have to cut our honeymoon short. Can't Donald handle this? Isn't that why you have an assistant pastor?"

Zachariah took a deep breath and stopped packing his t-shirts and shorts in his suitcase. Mary knew that he was going to try and reason with her, but it wasn't going to work. "I've got to get back and make sure that everything is okay."

She folded her arms across her chest. "But there's nothing you can do to change anything by rushing back to Atlanta. We've only got two more days. Why can't you just stay and go home when you are supposed to?"

"You know I won't be able to relax and enjoy myself here in Jamaica while I am thinking about all the damage to Mt. Zion," Zachariah said as he crossed the bedroom floor of their suite to move closer to his upset wife. But Mary stepped out of his reach. There was no way he could sweet talk his way out of this one.

"Listen. I know you are worried about the flood at your church. But didn't you say it was only in one bathroom? The plumber found the leak and the contractors already pulled up the tile floor that buckled and removed the mildewed cabinets. Can't you just pick out new floors and cabinets when we get back? We only get one honeymoon for God sake." Mary was trying not to whine, but she knew how stubborn her new husband could be once he made up his mind to do something.

Zachariah stared at Mary for a few seconds. She knew that he really didn't have time to argue with her if he was going to make the new flight that he had charged an arm and a leg on his credit card to get a seat on. "Stop using the Lord's name in vain. And I told you that it's our church now. Which means that you should be just as worried about it as I am. Plus the water went out into the hallway so, the carpet is going to have to be replaced out there too. Besides, Jamaica isn't going anywhere. We can always come back here."

Mary rolled her eyes and pouted. "When was the last time you took any time off?" Zachariah chuckled which made her angrier. "What's so funny?"

"I thought we left the grandkids at home. You look like April standing there about to have a temper tantrum." Mary spun around and slid the sliding glass door open that led to the balcony. She walked out to get a breath of fresh air and enjoy the peaceful ocean view. Her husband could rush back early if he wanted to. She was determined to stay right here in paradise and enjoy the rest of their honeymoon even if she had to do it alone. Suddenly Zachariah walked up behind her and gently grabbed her waist. "I'm sorry this happened while we were on vacation, but I've got to handle this myself. If Joshua were still the assistant pastor, I would have let him handle it, but he is not. It's not that easy to give up full control of my church to someone that I haven't known his entire life like my son."

She wiggled loose and turned around to face him. "It's our church, remember?" For the first time since his cell phone rang this morning with the news from Donald that one of the church's bathrooms had flooded, they shared a smile. "But I thought you said Donald was doing a great job so far and that you were happy with your selection of him to take Joshua's place?" He put his head down and sighed. It was Mary's turn to chuckle now. "For all your big talk about wanting to give up control of the church to the next generation and retire, you sure are holding on real tight."

"That was when I thought one of my sons was going to take over Mt. Zion." He backed up and exhaled. "It still hurts thinking that my dream of one of them walking in my footsteps and becoming senior pastor will never come true. But David would rather be minister of music and Joshua has his supper club now." He threw his hands up in the air and continued, "Donald is doing well, but he still needs lots of grooming."

Mary closed her eyes and shook her head. They hadn't even been married a week but she was already coming second to the church. Was this what being a first lady was going to be like? Reluctantly, she gave in and conceded to being on the losing end of their first official argument as husband and wife.

Zachariah lifted her chin and looked into her eyes. "Are you sure you don't want me to book you a ticket too? The kids aren't at the house so we can continue our honeymoon at home when I finish up handling business at the church." Any other time she would relish the thought of staring into the eyes of her handsome husband and giving into his every wish. But not today.

"As good as that offer sounds, I'm not ready to go back to reality yet. So I'm going to stay here and sign up for the tour of all the best places to shop in Montego Bay." Zachariah leaned his head back and looked up at the sky. "That's right. The tour you didn't want to go on because you said I would spend all the money we got as wedding gifts." He looked back at his wife and smiled as she continued taunting him. "And I'm going to sign up for as many services in the spa as my little heart desires." Mary shrugged her shoulders and smirked. "That's the price you pay when you leave your lovely wife alone for two days." The newlyweds sauntered back into their suite with their arms around each other's waists. But it wouldn't be long before he had to board the shuttle solo back to the airport en route to Hartsfield-Jackson Atlanta International Airport.

Mary thought about asking him to pick up her three grandkids from his son David's house as soon as the plane landed. She was sure that they had gotten on David and his wife Monica's nerves by now since they had a toddler of their own to worry about. It was a blessing that anyone had volunteered to babysit them for a week while they celebrated their new union at an all-inclusive beach resort. It was one thing for April to follow David's direction while she was singing in his choir at rehearsals and on Sunday mornings, but April could be very rebellious with authority figures when she didn't want to do something they told her to do. But why bother? If she knew her husband, Pastor Zachariah Williams would spend the majority of his time at the church until it was time to pick her up from the airport in a couple of days. The kids would be at home but alone with April, the sixteen-year-old, in charge. Her firstborn grandchild had matured a lot since their mother Felicia got arrested and Mary became their unofficial guardian. But Anthony Jr. at fourteen and Brooklyn at eleven didn't like being told what to do by April anymore now that their grandmother was around. So the three of them were better off where they were. Hopefully, they were behaving for their new aunt and uncle.

She turned her attention back to her husband. Offering to finish packing for him, he jumped in the shower and got dressed for his nearly three-hour flight. He left the bathroom door open so she could enjoy the view, but she heard him turn the water off when his cell rang. Zachariah had made six phone calls since he got the news a couple hours ago. Listening to him talk on his phone in the bathroom, she realized that he was right. He would get on her last nerve worrying about the damage from the flood if he stayed. Other than answering a few emails from his cell phone in the last five days, she had managed to keep his mind off his job while they enjoyed all the activities that Sandals had to offer. But all of that had come to an abrupt end with one call from home. Although she was furious about her honeymoon being ruined, it didn't make any sense for her to be upset with Donald for too long. If he didn't call, Zachariah would have been furious with him once he got home and no one notified him about the flood immediately.

An hour later, the couple was walking from their room through the garden to the front of the resort so he could catch the airport shuttle. They exchanged a quick hug and a kiss before Zachariah hopped on the shuttle. She shook her head but wasn't going to let his rushed kiss upset her any more than she already was. Besides, she had things to do. Mary went straight to the front desk to sign up for the all-day shopping tour. Then she made a beeline to the spa to sign up for a facial and a deep tissue massage tomorrow so she would be refreshed when she returned back to the real world.

Mary looked around at all the happy couples walking hand in hand. Some were probably on their way to activities at the private beach. Others were headed to one of the many restaurants the resort offered. She was adamant about her decision to stay, but quickly realized that there would be no more candle lit dinners on the beach with the tide tickling their feet. And no more participating in the couples billiards contest or duo beach volleyball matches that had been so much fun. Suddenly feeling lonely, Mary retreated back to the suite for some room service. Their exciting honeymoon in paradise was officially over.

2

Zachariah was glad that his life could finally get back to normal. All the stress of planning the wedding, making honeymoon arrangements, buying and selling houses, getting her grandkids into a new school, and moving was finally behind him. When he married his first wife they didn't have any money, so they got married in her parents' living room in front of the fireplace and had a small reception right there in her family's backyard. Everyone in both families chipped in so they could spend a couple days in a hotel in Savannah for their honeymoon. And they returned from the honeymoon to their tiny one-bedroom apartment. He had come a long way since then.

Mary and Zachariah both wanted a ceremony at Mt. Zion. But that was the only thing they agreed on. Zachariah didn't think they needed to go all out since this was a second marriage for both of them. But Mary didn't see it that way. She didn't have the money to have a lavish wedding her first time around either, but she planned to make up for it this time. So Zachariah gave in to make his future wife happy. He figured the planning would keep her busy and out of his way for several months simply touching bases with him for the money she needed.

Unfortunately, someone put it in her head that today's grooms helped their brides with the wedding planning. So she was always pulling him away from church business to go to a wedding appointment. Mary was the definition of an overbearing bride with all of her demands for the reception and honeymoon. If he said he wanted a DJ, she'd say they needed a band. If he said he wanted the ceremony to start at three o'clock, she would say she wanted it to start at five o'clock. His opinion didn't seem to matter, but she would get upset and say he didn't care about the wedding if he didn't have something to say about every little detail. He didn't even want to go to Jamaica. Atlanta was hot enough in the summer, why go somewhere even hotter? He thought they should go on a cruise. That way they could dock at several different islands and still be inside a nice cool ship the majority of the time. But Mary was afraid she would get seasick. She insisted that they go to an island resort instead and he ended up giving in again to keep the peace.

At the same time that they were planning the

wedding and honeymoon, they were also house hunting. Zachariah didn't see anything wrong with hiring a moving company to help Mary and the kids pack up her house and move it to his house. But once again, his future wife wasn't going for that idea. She refused to move into his house. When he mentioned their disagreement to his assistant pastor Donald he said, "Even I know that you can't ask your new wife to move into your first wife's house."

Donald had a good point. That and the thought of continuing to walk up and down all those stairs at his house were the only reasons that he agreed to sell his house. As long as they had a master bedroom on the main level and he didn't have to maneuver any stairs for the next twenty years, he would move. But because Mary was getting everything she wanted and he wasn't getting anything he asked for even though he was paying for everything, he put his foot down and insisted that he get to stay in his neighborhood. He told her flat out, "If you aren't willing to give me this one request, then you aren't the woman for me." Mary wasn't happy, but he finally won an argument.

Now that he was back in town and had taken care of the flood at the church and some other pressing Mt. Zion business, he was on his laptop catching up on emails. They were mostly church related, but a few were congratulation emails from people who couldn't make it to the wedding or reception. The messages reminded him of Mary and the disappointed look on her face when he left her in Jamaica. He loved his new family, but Mt. Zion was his life's work. No one could take care of it like he could. As a minister, he had to make sacrifices. Now that she was first lady, Mary was going to have to make sacrifices too and get used to sharing him with the entire congregation. Hopefully, she understood why he had to leave and wasn't still upset with him when he picked her up from the airport tomorrow. He decided that he'd better stop at the store and buy her a welcome home gift just to be sure.

As far as tonight, he was going to enjoy the peace and quiet of his last night in an empty house. Which is why he decided to wait until he picked up Mary before he went to get the kids. Despite what his wife thought, he knew his son Donald could handle them. He always wanted a house full of kids of his own. One week with the rambunctious Lewis kids would either make him totally change his mind or leave him feeling like he could fly like Superman.

Making the decision to ask Mary to marry him was an easy one. She was beautiful. All of her curves were exactly where they needed to be. She was smart and had always been there as a support system for him. He loved to be around her because she was easy to talk to. But being sixty with teenagers and a preteen wasn't easy. Now that they were all going to be living in the same house, he was going to experience first-hand the things that Mary complained over the phone to him about. He knew that if Mary had been consistently in their lives they probably wouldn't act the way they did. April was rebellious. Anthony Jr. was withdrawn. And Brooklyn was needy. Their behavior was all very different, yet they all stemmed from having a father who abandoned them running from the police and a mother who used drugs to cope with life after he disappeared. Mary was able to give them a stable loving home. And he was ready to do everything in his power to back her up. He knew that it would be weird for him to have a house full of kids again. It may take some adjusting for them to get used to a man being in the house again too. But they all loved Mary and she wanted to make this family work. He wanted his new wife to be happy.

The kids were definitely rough around the edges though, especially April. Mary told him about the times that she overheard her talking on the phone to friends. "She didn't know that I was behind her and every other word that came out of that child's mouth was a curse word. I didn't know girls spoke like that to each other. If my mother had heard me swearing like that, she would have washed my mouth out with soap."

As a minister with a church in a poor area of town, Zachariah witnessed and heard all types of ghetto behavior. So April's cursing, fighting, and even getting caught having sex at school in a closet didn't surprise him like it did Mary. His wife had a hard time accepting that her daughter Felicia and her granddaughter's lives weren't turning out the way she hoped that they would. Like his sons did for instance. But he knew that April, Jr., and Brooklyn didn't have the benefit of living in a nice neighborhood or attending a private school all their lives like Joshua and David did. Zachariah hoped that his positive presence in the house would help refine them before it was too late.

When Zachariah got home that evening, he realized that aside from the few canned goods that were in the cabinets, they didn't have any food. He remembered Mary stating that it didn't make sense to go grocery shopping since they would be on their honeymoon for a week and the kids would be at David's house. She promised to go shopping to fill up the refrigerator and cabinets once they got back. Instead of going back out, he picked up the phone and ordered a pizza and a liter of orange soda to be delivered. He hooked up the TV, VHS player, and the stereo in the living room while he waited for the delivery guy to arrive.

Next, he opened up a few moving boxes with his personal belongings in them. He put his cologne bottles, watches, and cufflinks on his side of the dresser. Then he pulled out a silver framed picture of his first wife Gloria and put it on the corner of the dresser where it belonged. Then it hit him. He would no longer be able to look at her picture again every morning when he stood in the mirror like he had done every day since she passed away. It felt like she was looking at him as he dressed and giving her approval. Suddenly wondering what he would do if he couldn't see her everyday anymore, Zachariah decided to leave her picture there until tomorrow. That way, he would have one last morning with her and she could see that he was doing fine. Before he left to get his new family, he would put her safely away in his drawer so Mary wouldn't be upset.

About twenty minutes later, the doorbell finally rang. After he tipped the young man, Zachariah kicked off his shoes and enjoyed his sausage and pepperoni pizza reclining on the couch watching TV. A quick glance at the news showed President George H. W. Bush speaking about

Clarence Thomas, his nomination to the Supreme Court to replace Thurgood Marshall. He kept pressing the remote in search of a sports channel.

If Mary were here she would fuss about him not eating any vegetables and drinking a soda. Ever since his heart attack last year, she tried to dictate what he ate as much as possible. Now that they were living together and she would be cooking for him every day, he imagined his freedom to eat whatever he wanted was over. But he was a grown man and his wife wasn't there today. She was still in Jamaica spending up all their wedding money. So he could eat whatever he wanted. He laughed out loud at himself because despite his rebelliousness, he fully intended to pass right by the kitchen trash can, throw the empty pizza box and bottle of soda outside, and hope that Mary didn't find any evidence that it had ever been there.

3

April's grandmother and new grandfather finally picked her and her siblings up from her new Uncle David's house. Even though it was only a week, it seemed like they were there forever. They had a pretty house in a nice neighborhood with a lot of space, but it was only a three-bedroom house. David and his wife shared the master bedroom. Their baby was in his nursery. So that left one guest bedroom. Anthony got to sleep on a pullout sofa in the fully remodeled basement, while April was once again stuck sleeping with her little sister. As soon as they moved into their house that her grandmother and grandfather bought, it was time for them to go on their honeymoon before April could even sleep in her new bed.

She hated spending her last week before school

started staying at someone else's house. But her grandmother had jammed the move, her wedding, and their honeymoon all in the summer so they wouldn't occur during the school year. April was happy for her grandmother, but it seemed like the entire summer had been about the adults. Now the summer was almost over and it was time to go back to school. She didn't even get to enjoy her summer vacation. Her grandmother dragged her to cake tastings, dress fittings, and meetings with her wedding coordinator as if she was actually interested in wedding planning. Her grandmother chose to only have family in their wedding party. So she treated April as her maid of honor. All April could think was, *who would actually like being bossed around and having to do all this wedding crap for someone else?* And now, she had to sit and listen to the details of the fun the adults had on their vacation on a tropical island. Wasn't summertime supposed to be vacation time for kids?

"Grandma, did you have fun?"

"Yes, Brooklyn, we had a good time."

"Do they have the same TV shows over there in Jamaica?"

Mary looked at Zachariah and chuckled. "I don't know sweetie. We never even turned on the TV."

"That's disgusting. Nobody wants to hear all that Grandma," April objected.

Pastor cleared his throat and glared at April sitting in the backseat of his black Mercedes Benz through the

22

rearview mirror. Grandma hurried to clear up the misunderstanding. "That's not what I meant. We were too busy enjoying the resort to watch any TV."

"Well what did you do there?" Brooklyn continued her interrogation.

"The resort had plenty of activities for us to choose from. We went out on a boat, played tennis, competed in couples events, they had live bands and we ate at different restaurants every night."

"Grandma, we went to a few restaurants, too. 'Cause Uncle David said they aren't used to cooking dinner for so many people."

April let out a loud sigh. "Brooklyn she wasn't talking about McDonald's and Wendy's like we went to. They went to nice restaurants."

Their grandmother looked over her shoulder at her oldest grandchild. "What's wrong with you young lady? You've had an attitude since we picked you up."

"Grandma, she's been acting like this all week," Brooklyn announced. "Everyone, even the baby got in the pool in their backyard the other day. But April wouldn't get in. She said she didn't want to get her hair wet. And all of us watched movies together, but she never wanted to watch what we were watching."

Rolling her eyes, April denied that anything was wrong with her. Her grandmother turned back and faced the road. No one said anything for a few minutes until

Grandma broke the silence. "We are going back-to-school shopping tomorrow. I'm going to buy your uniforms and some school supplies."

"How are we going shopping for school supplies and we haven't even gone to school yet? You don't even know what we need."

Zachariah's booming voice made April's body jerk. "Watch your tone young lady. Somebody wants to buy you something that you need and all you want to do is complain?"

April raised her eyebrow and stared at the back of his head. She didn't want Pastor to think now that he was married to her grandmother he could start chastising her too. So she had to let him know that she wasn't going to stop talking just because he didn't like what she was saying. "I'm just saying. How are we going to know what we need before our teachers tell us?"

Her grandmother reached over and rubbed his right arm. Then she cut him off before he could respond. "I was buying school supplies before you were even born, little girl. Besides, the academy emailed me a list of what the three of you need in your new student packet. You need new book bags, filler paper, spiral notebooks, markers, glue, pens and pencils."

Anthony Jr. had been sitting quietly playing on his Game Boy not interested in the conversation going on around him. Suddenly he blurted out, "Can I get the new Jordans that just came out?"

Grandma looked over her other shoulder. "Well look who finally decided to snap out of his trance. I've been gone a week and barely got a hello from you young man."

A smirk spread across Anthony's lips. "Hey Grandma. I had to finish my game and I didn't want to get killed." He paused for a second, but quickly asked again, "So can I?"

"Can you what?" she asked.

"Can I get the new Air Jordans that just came out when we go back-to-school shopping, Grandma?"

"I don't know. We'll see."

Zachariah turned to Mary and asked, "Didn't you say he could only play his games on the weekends?"

April could see the side of her grandmother's face scrunch up when she turned back around. "Yes, but it is still summertime, baby. Things will be back to normal as soon as school starts."

Anthony Jr. and April didn't get along most of the time, but when he turned to face her, April knew that they were thinking the exact same thing. Pastor was going to be a problem. She rationalized that he was new to their family and they were going to have to show him his place. Sure if he wanted to throw some allowance money her way she wouldn't object. But as far as him stepping in and trying to change the routine that the four of them had developed over the last year, she was determined not to let that happen.

25

April was confident that her little brother had her back. She wasn't sure about her goody-two-shoes little sister though. Brooklyn seemed to worship the ground that Pastor walked on.

4

It felt so good pulling up the circular driveway with her family and seeing her shiny new silver Jaguar XJ parked in front of their 3,950 square-foot, five-bedroom home. Her car was a wedding present from her husband. He surprised her with it the day before the wedding at rehearsal since it was tradition for the groom not to see his bride before the wedding on their wedding day. She spent ten minutes crying and hugging him before she was finally able to slide in the driver seat of the luxury vehicle she had dreamed about owning for twenty years. The car was a surprise, but they picked out this house together. Even though her old house was closer to the church, it was too small for her and the kids as it was. And although he didn't come out and say it, Mary knew that he would never move in it anyway. He claimed to be down to Earth, but he was used to so much more. Zachariah had assumed that she and the kids would move into his house. But Mary told him, as tactfully as she could, that she could never live in a house that he purchased for another woman. So they put their two houses on the market and began the search for a new home.

She had to admit that Zachariah owned a beautiful house. So his sold quickly. But after a few months and a reduction in price, Mary's home was still on the market. Her house was paid for, so it wasn't as if they were paying two mortgages. Mary was content with it remaining on the market until she got a fair price for it. She wasn't going to just give away something that it had taken her all of her adult life to pay for.

As adamant as Mary was about not living in another woman's house, even though she had loved the original first lady herself, Zachariah was equally as unwavering about remaining in his same neighborhood. Their new home was only six blocks from his old house. As a matter of fact, they had to drive past his old street to get to their home. Mary felt a little leery about that. It seemed like he was trying his best to hang on to his dead wife in any way he could. All of the subdivisions in this area off Cascade Road were lined with nice homes. So why did they have to be so close to his old house? But Mary quickly gave in because it was the prettiest house that she had ever seen in her entire life. It was a big step up from her tiny home. She imagined that she could put her old house inside this house twice and still have room. It was love at first sight when she saw that the huge kitchen had all stainless steel appliances, two ovens, and a walk-in pantry. The master bedroom was on the main level like Zachariah wanted. The previous owners had thought of everything for the entire family in the basement. They built a home theater, a game room for kids, and a den that was perfect as a man cave. The yard had wonderful curb appeal. And the best part was that the kids had the entire three-bedroom top level of the house all to themselves. April and Brooklyn would share the Jack and Jill bathroom while Anthony Jr. would have his own bathroom down the hall. Mary only intended to walk up their flight of stairs once a day. That was to get them up for school in the mornings.

One of the reasons that Mary fell in love with Zachariah was because they had so much in common. Both of their spouses had passed away within a year of each other. Her husband died first so she knew how crushed he was when his wife lost her fight with breast cancer. They became closer friends because she spent so much time volunteering at his church. As she assisted him in his office at the church, they were able to help each other heal from the pain of the death of their loved ones. It was inevitable that they would fall in love because they were both easy to talk to and fun to be around. But most of all, they both loved the Lord and spent a lot of their time devoted to Mt. Zion.

Another reason she fell in love was his willingness to help her with her grandchildren. When she'd first gotten the call from her daughter to go get her kids because she was in jail, Mary had a lot of adjusting to do getting used to having three kids around. But he was always available to listen to her vent and offer suggestions on how to fix the problems that she was having, especially with April. He had even forgiven April when she falsely accused his son of molesting her. She had a crush on Joshua and overheard him complaining about how much of a problem child she was and wanted revenge, so she lied.

They had all weathered that storm and the scandal that it had caused in the church together. He had even been willing to buy a house big enough for all of them. So she wasn't sure what Zachariah's newfound attitude with the children was about now that they were back from the honeymoon and settling into the house with the kids. He hadn't had one nice thing to say to them since they had picked them up from David's house. She intended to find out what he was upset about later tonight when they were alone. But right now they needed to unload everyone's luggage from the car. Then she needed to run to the grocery store and get started cooking dinner for her family in their new top of the line top-of-the-line kitchen.

Later that evening, Mary entered their bedroom and closed the door behind her. Zachariah was propped up on their king size bed with his laptop on his lap and a notebook next to him. She didn't like the fact that he brought his work home with him. He had been working all day at the church and now he was still working at nine o'clock at night. When he had his heart attack last year, his doctor advised him to change his lifestyle. He was supposed to modify his eating habits which meant cutting back on fast food, fried food, and the excessive amount of junk food that he ate instead of a healthy meal. Mary was going to be helping him with that part of bettering his life since she was cooking for him now. His cardiologist also suggested that he exercise and cut down on the long hours at Mt. Zion. She had not been successful at getting him to work out or cut down on his stress level though. He usually made an excuse when she wanted to exercise and he was an undeniable workaholic especially since he had to take a new assistant pastor under his wing.

"Are you okay today baby?"

"I'm fine. Why'd you ask me that?"

Mary walked over to her dresser and glanced at him through the reflection in the mirror. She pulled off her earrings and said, "You were being a little rough on the kids earlier."

Zachariah looked up from his computer for the first time. "You can't let April talk to you like that. And all that boy does is play video games. We need to sign him up for sports. Does he like football or basketball?"

Mary sucked in her bottom lip and turned to face him. "I don't know. Guess I've been preoccupied with the wedding and moving lately to think about anything else."

"Well we need to set some rules and decide how they will be punished if they don't follow them. These kids need chores and extracurricular activities to keep them busy and out of trouble."

"Baby, you act like the kids walk all over me or something."

Zachariah chuckled. "You have eased up on them this summer." He kept the smile on his face and motioned for her to come closer. By the time she made it to his side of the bed he had shut the laptop and pushed it to the other side of the bed to make room for her. "But I can understand that you were preoccupied about marrying the man of your dreams and all."

Mary couldn't hide the big grin that spread across her face. "Man of my dreams, huh? You are mighty sure of yourself aren't you, Mr. Williams?"

He pulled her down on the bed next to him. "I'm sure that we were meant to be together. That's what I'm sure of. And I'm sure that these kids outnumber us three to two so we have to have a united front. Felicia is your only child so you don't know how siblings will stick together and try to run the household. You know they think that they are younger and smarter than us, right Mrs. Williams?"

"Well they've got the part about being younger than us correct." Mary exhaled. "But I understand what you are saying. You are the man of the house. We do have to establish new rules for our house." Mary flung her hands up in the air, "But I want them to like you, baby."

"I'm from the old school. They just need to respect me, do what I say and everything will be fine. If not, then we are going to have problems." Zachariah paused and then began to smile at his wife. "Are we going to talk about the kids all night?"

Mary could tell by the sheepish grin on his face that he had other things on his mind right now. She matched his smile with one of her own and quickly answered, "Absolutely not."

Her sexy husband smiled at her and just like that, all of the tension disappeared. "Hold that thought. I have a surprise for you."

She couldn't help the big goofy smile that spread across her face. His words were magic to her ears after the turbulent flight back home alone, April's nasty attitude, and the crowded grocery store today.

"Close your eyes."

With her eyes closed she could hear the wooden dresser drawer creak open and shut. She was expecting her new husband to instruct her to put on some new lingerie or something. Instead her mouth dropped when she opened her eyes to a tiny velvet box with sparkling diamond earrings. Mary looked up to her husband with questioning tear-filled eyes.

"I wanted to get you a gift to apologize for leaving you in Jamaica. I chose diamonds because they are indestructible just like our love."

Hands down, that was the most romantic thing anyone had ever said to her.

5

It was a quiet Sunday morning. As far as she knew, Mary was the only one awake in the house. Today was her first Sunday service as the new first lady of Mt. Zion Baptist Church. So she spent the night tossing and turning without getting any sleep. She yawned as she flipped over the last few pieces of bacon in the pan. The grits were almost ready so she added a heaping tablespoon of butter and a handful of shredded extra sharp cheddar cheese to the pot. Zachariah nearly made her burn herself when he snuck up behind her and patted her on her behind. "I knew I smelled something good cooking in here."

Mary jumped and grabbed her chest. "You won't get to eat it if you have to drive me to the emergency room. You almost made me burn myself." She giggled and tried to swat his hand away as he stole a piece of bacon off the napkin next to the stove but he was too quick for her. He gave her a wet kiss on her cheek and all was forgiven. "Baby, can you yell upstairs and tell the kids that breakfast is ready before you leave?"

"Okay. Then I'm headed out the door for the first service. See you in a little while." He took off in the direction of the stairs leading to the kids' rooms.

One of the major changes that Donald initiated as the new assistant pastor of the church was having two Sunday services instead of one. He convinced Zachariah that he would have a full house at both services because some people loved getting up and going to church early to start their day. Soon after, they found that men like going to an earlier service so they wouldn't miss watching sports on TV. And when they started advertising two services, people that didn't come because the church had gotten too crowded began to come back. If Mary didn't have the kids to be concerned with, she would stay for both services with her husband. Instead, she only attended the second service because that is the one the kids were used to.

A few minutes later, Brooklyn was the first one to come skipping down to the kitchen still wearing her pink robe and matching pajamas. "Good morning young lady."

"Good morning Grandma. Do we have any orange juice?"

"I'm sure we do. Look in the fridge."

Just then Anthony came around the corner and

pushed Brooklyn out of the refrigerator to get himself some juice.

"Hey," Brooklyn yelled and pushed her big brother back. "Did you see that Grandma?"

April arrived just in time to steal the glass of juice out of her brother's hand.

Mary wiped the sweat from her forehead and neck. She turned toward the commotion behind the fridge and announced, "We don't have time for any foolishness this morning y'all."

A few minutes later, the four of them had fixed their plates and were sitting at the kitchen table enjoying breakfast together. Mary chewed the last bite of her food, looked at Anthony and Brooklyn and said, "We're going to be sitting on the front row now so I need you two to be on your best behavior."

They quickly looked at each other. Brooklyn was the first to speak. "You mean we get to sit on the pew at the front of the church because we are part of Pastor's family now?" Mary smiled and nodded. "You hear that Anthony? That means you can't mess with me anymore because Grandma, Pastor, and the whole entire church will see you." Anthony rolled his eyes and kept shoveling grits in his mouth. Brooklyn stood up and announced, "I'm going to pick out a cute dress for my first time on the front row." Everyone shook their heads or laughed at her as she ran upstairs.

April pouted. "That's not fair. Nobody is going to

see what I have on under my choir robe."

Mary realized that she wanted to pick out something extra special for her first time on the front pew of the church as well. She quickly excused herself from the table and headed straight to her walk-in closet pushing clothes around on the rack to pick out her Sunday bests.

An hour and a half later, the family was pulling into the parking lot of the church as cars were pulling out from the last service. Mary had a huge smile on her face as she was directed by the attendant to pull into the parking spot in front of Mt. Zion that read Parking for First Lady Williams. "Grandma, did they put those balloons on the sign for you?" Brooklyn peered out the window and asked.

"No stupid. They put a bunch of balloons on a sign for the First Lady for someone else," Anthony answered sarcastically as April laughed loudly.

Mary stopped smiling, squinted her eyes and stared at him, "Did you forget what I said about being on your best behavior?"

"But she asked a really stupid question."

Mary noticed that the parking attendant was still standing by the car and realized that he was waiting to help her out. She quickly aimed the rearview mirror down to do a last minute check of her lipstick. "Okay. Let's go inside." She smiled at him and he opened her car door and extended his hand to assist her out of her car. "Thank you."

"My pleasure, First Lady Williams."

Mary liked the sound of that. *I am First Lady Williams.*

The ushers opened the doors and greeted the family. Mary walked up to Zachariah's office with all three children close behind her like a line of ducks. She planned to wait with him in his office until it was time for their entrance. But apparently April had other plans. "Can I go wait with the choir? I'm not walking in with the family anyway." Mary said yes and April took off in the other direction. She knocked on the door, but then walked right in without waiting for his reply. Inside they found him talking to Donald.

"Good morning."

"Good morning First Lady." Donald stood up out of respect. "Did you see that we got the flood all taken care of? Everything is as good as new."

With all the excitement of the day, she had totally forgotten all about the disaster that prematurely ended her honeymoon. "Oh." Mary shrugged. "I'm sorry. I hadn't even noticed anything new." She looked at her watch and noticed that they still had a few more minutes before the service started.

"Well I'll be in my office until service begins if you need me Pastor."

Closing the door behind him, Donald waved to the kids and left the office.

"What was that about? You were rude to him for no

reason," Zachariah stated.

Mary averted her eyes from his. "I just think that he could have handled it himself. Our honeymoon didn't have to be disturbed."

"We've talked about this before. It wasn't his fault. I chose to come back and handle the situation myself." He put his hand up to stop her from responding. "I'm working here Mary. I don't need this right now." He glanced over at the kids frozen against the wall and then back at her as a reminder that they were still not alone in the room. He softened his tone and stated, "I haven't seen the two of you this quiet before." Suddenly it was clear to the adults that the children had never heard them arguing before and didn't know what to do.

Mary motioned for Brooklyn to come closer. She slowly moved further into the room and Mary smoothed down her hair and kissed her on the cheek. "Grandma, we should go so we won't be late."

"No honey. We have to wait until church starts before we go in now. After the choir sings a few songs, we'll follow Pastor in and sit down."

Brooklyn looked at Pastor for confirmation and protested when he agreed. "That's not fair. The singing is the best part of church. I don't understand why we have to stay back here and miss it."

"Baby, you can hear the singing from here."

"Yes, but I can't see the choir." Brooklyn pouted

FATHER, CAN YOU HEAR ME?

and plopped down in the chair next to her grandmother with her arms folded across her chest. "And what if April gets to sing a solo? Do I have to stay back here then, too?"

Mary leaned towards Zachariah and whispered, "She's got a point. What if me and the kids go in when the choir sings their first song? We don't need to make a grand entrance. Everyone needs to be looking at you, not us anyway."

"That's not the way we do it Mary."

She rolled her eyes. They landed over at the bookcase and immediately noticed a picture of him and his first wife. She wanted to tell him that's not the way he used to do it with his deceased wife, but things were different now. Mary fumbled in her purse for a tissue to wipe her neck with. *What a horrible time to be having my own private summer.* Too antsy to sit down, Mary walked over to the bookcase to see what pictures she needed to replace. Suddenly she heard, "Whatever Mary." When Zachariah got up from his desk, Mary thought he was coming to give her a kiss. Instead he removed the picture of his first wife from her hand.

All eyes were on Mary as she and the kids walked in the sanctuary as the choir sang their first song. Several members, including the deacons, stood up out of respect until they took their seats. Surprisingly, Anthony behaved himself. And Mary and Brooklyn got to enjoy the choir singing. Mary really looked at her husband as he walked up the steps to his pulpit. He looked so sharp with his tailored gray suit that hugged his upper body. And he was all hers.

Their argument a few minutes ago seems insignificant now.

Soon it was time for the church announcements. When the announcements were over, Donald invited Mary up to the podium and asked Zachariah to join her. She reluctantly walked up on stage and looked at her husband for answers. He shrugged his shoulders to let her know that he didn't know what was going on either. Mary looked out into the congregation at all the different shades of melanin as everyone stared back at her. She was so nervous about anyone noticing her body shaking that she couldn't focus on what the assistant pastor was saying. Then she realized that he and a couple members of the deacon board were unveiling a life-size oil painting of the two of them. It was the same pose that they had on the huge billboard outside the church. Mary concentrated just in time to hear. "We commissioned Brother Thomas to paint this for you as a wedding present from the church."

Mary loved the billboard that was right outside the church. Zachariah told her that he also replaced the one on the other side of town. It made her proud that their love was on display for the entire city to see. But now that their images were captured forever in this painting, she was extremely moved. In her mind, she said a thank you Jesus that she decided to wear the royal blue dress that made her look ten pounds slimmer than she was. She was also pleased with her choice of the outfit that she picked for her husband. He looked very distinguished with his salt and pepper hair and matching beard in his navy suit with gray pinstripes. Their forms popped against the light textured background of the portrait.

With tears in her eyes Mary thanked the men in front of her. Zachariah took the microphone and thanked the entire congregation for their generous gift and spoke about how talented the painter was. She shook her head in agreement. The artist had done a beautiful job on the painting. It was understood that the painting was to be hung in the foyer at Mt. Zion, but Mary desperately wanted to hang the painting in their home. She made a mental note to speak to the artist about doing a smaller piece to put over the fireplace in their living room.

After another stirring sermon from Zachariah, ten more people joined the church. Mary was so amazed that he always came up with things to preach about week after week, year after year. She always loved looking up at the pulpit and listening to him address his flock. This morning, she literally had a front row seat and she couldn't be more proud to be his wife.

At the end of service, it seemed like the entire congregation stuck around to hug and congratulate the happy couple. Mary had to admit that she loved all of this new attention she was getting as first lady of the church. She felt like she was finally living the good life everyone dreams about.

6

April looked forward to making it to the high school down the street once she finally graduated a year late from middle school back in May. But all of that went out the window when her grandmother married Pastor and they moved to a different neighborhood. Now, all three of them were enrolled in Grove Wood Academy. It was a private school that went from pre-k through twelfth grade. They were all in different buildings. Brooklyn was in the lower school, Anthony in the middle school, and April was in the upper school. But they were on the same campus and April wasn't happy about being at the same school as her siblings again. And on top of that, they had to wear stupid school uniforms every day. The short sleeve Polo style cotton shirts had three buttons, folded down collars, and the school name in small letters on them. The boys wore khaki pants and the girls had the choice of wearing khaki pants or a khaki pleated skirt with solid knee-high socks. April hadn't been able to go wild buying school clothes since her dad was around. Now that her grandmother had the money to shop as the wife of a pastor, April still wouldn't be able to go clothes shopping. The only thing she could freely pick out was her shoes.

Her grandmother and Pastor didn't even ask them if they wanted to go to school there. One day they sat her and her siblings down and announced that they had already paid the three application fees and began the process for them to attend the school. Unbeknownst to April, they had contacted their schools and gotten records of their grades and references from teachers and church members for them. The only thing the three of them had to do was complete an essay.

Despite her and Anthony's questions and protest, it had already been decided that if they were accepted, they were going. Brooklyn was the only one excited about it. Apparently one of her friends from church was a student there so she was eager to attend. But her little sister was a bonafide nerd, so her opinion didn't count to April or Anthony Jr.

That night, April studied the pamphlets for the academy and saw a few pictures of African American and Latino students, but for the most part the kids were all White. There were only a few White kids at her old school, because Whites were the minority at Sojourner Truth Middle School. Some of the kids called them poor White trash while others were cool with them because they said they acted Black. But April didn't have any classes with them and never felt the need to interact with the White kids. All of the young people at Mt. Zion were Black. So she didn't even know how Caucasian kids acted. Most of the White children that she saw were on TV. They seemed rich and stuck up to her.

She had a few nonblack school teachers over the years. They taught as well as the African American ones, but they seemed less confident when it came to disciplining the kids. Students talked in code or slang in their classrooms and the out of place minority in the room didn't know what they were saying, but the African American educators did because they were from the same culture. Students were more likely to be able to walk all over a White teacher at her school than they were a Black one. April figured it was because the Black teachers probably came from the hood themselves, so they weren't scared of them or their parents. But a White teacher from the other side of town would be.

April had seen quite a few angry parents coming up to the school to confront teachers. She remembered being in elementary school on an important testing day. Their Caucasian instructor let the entire class go to the lavatory and let them know that no one would be able to leave the room again during the test. When one of the girls started squirming at her desk and begged to go to the restroom, the teacher told her that she would have to wait. A few minutes later, the little girl jumped up and ran out of the room headed to the bathroom anyway and didn't return. About an hour later, her mother stormed her way into April's classroom threatening to beat the teacher up because her daughter peed on herself. April remembered seeing the fear in her White teacher's face as a male teacher and a security guard had to restrain the loud parent and drag her out of the classroom. The woman was arrested and charged with terroristic threats. April had never seen a parent threaten a Black teacher like that. And she hadn't seen a parent get arrested for arguing with an African American instructor either. She wondered if it was all about race.

The only real interaction that she had with a White person was her psychiatrist. April still went to see her twice a month ever since her school recommended that she take medication for her behavior. At first, April couldn't stand her. Eventually, she began to grow on her like gospel which was her favorite music now. Her office was a safe place to discuss all of April's problems and not have to worry about the doctor telling anyone what was discussed. Sometimes she even had very good advice for April. Although she would never admit it to her grandmother, occasionally April even checked the calendar to see how many more days until she got to go see her therapist. She wondered if her experience with other White people would be like this.

Looking at the pamphlet, April also noticed how much the tuition was. In her opinion, it was ridiculous to pay for school when they could go to school a lot closer to home for free. She didn't see anything wrong with public schools. If her grandmother and Pastor wanted to spend ten thousand dollars per child, April could think of a whole lot better things they could buy her than a high school education. Pastor must make a lot more money at Mt. Zion than she thought he did. Since he made so much money, April decided that when the time was right she was going to ask for a weekly allowance.

Their first day of school came too soon. April looked around at her surroundings and knew that she wasn't going to like this stuffy place. Three students were at the flagpole raising the American flag when her family marched up the walkway to the front door. Other kids were posted in the hallway wearing orange sashes across their chest as if they were policing the hallway activity. Teachers and administrators were also standing in the doorway of their classrooms and the doorway to the upper school office. April looked through the sea of white faces and saw one Black teacher.

The only thing she was going to like about this school was that it was thirty minutes away from the house. Now that she is sixteen, her grandmother had given April her old car so that she could drive herself and brother and sister to school every day. She said it was just to drive to school and back. But she knew that her grandmother hated chauffeuring them around, especially when she had some place else to go. April figured it wouldn't be long before she was driving her car anytime she wanted to.

As for today, her grandmother had insisted on taking them to school herself. So April had been to three of the four buildings with her grandmother as she dropped off

Brooklyn and Jr. From what she had gathered from the pamphlets, the primary school building was for the youngest kids in pre-k through third grade. That was the only building they didn't have to enter as their grandmother dropped each of them off one by one. If her grandmother moved forward as if she was going to kiss her in front of all these people, like she did her little sister, April was going to be mortified. Thank goodness she had sense enough not to embarrass her.

When April entered the classroom, she immediately noticed all of the desktop computers at the tables on the other side of the room. There had to be at least twelve computers. She wondered if all of the rooms had this many devices. In her old school, they were lucky if each class had one or two computers. And if they actually worked, they were ten years old, loaded at a snail's pace, and had missing or broken keys.

She also noticed that she was the only Black student in this room. So she headed straight to the back row to get away from the teacher and everyone else. But this tactic didn't work. "Hi. I'm Robin. What's your name?" April stared at the chubby perky White girl with brunette hair staring down at her and wondered why she was talking to her. And she had the nerve to have her hand extended like she wanted them to shake hands like this was a business meeting or something.

"I'm April." Robin put down her hand once she realized that April wasn't going to shake it. There were several empty seats scattered around the room, yet Robin chose to sit right next to April. She looked around the room and noticed the other kids talking and laughing. They seemed to be reuniting with their classmates after a long summer without each other. No one was looking in their direction.

"What school did you come from?"

"Sojourner Truth Middle School," April flatly answered.

Robin was quiet for a few seconds. "I've never heard of that one."

"Of course you haven't. You've probably never been south of Midtown either." April peered over at her out of the corner of her eye waiting for Robin to defend herself, but she didn't. A minute later, the teacher entered from her post at the doorway and told everyone to have a seat so class could begin.

At lunchtime, April got her tray and headed to a secluded table. The teachers and students were nice enough to her so far, but she wasn't interested in being friends with any of them. She wanted to do her time there every day and get out without any incidents. The last thing she needed was her car taken away from her before she could enjoy it.

Not sixty seconds after she sat down at a table in the back of the lunchroom, Robin found her and sat down across from her without even asking. "So how is your first day going so far?" Before April could answer, Robin was on to the next question. "What class do you have next? I hope we have more than one class together." April sighed and slid Robin her schedule. "Oh great. We've got Theatre class together at the end of the day." She rolled her eyes and kept quiet. Apparently Robin was determined to make April be her friend whether she wanted her to or not. But April thought about it and maybe it would be good to have someone to help her navigate her way through this new place after all. So April ate and Robin occasionally paused to put a forkful of food in her mouth. She had never met anyone who talked more than her little sister Brooklyn until today.

When her grueling first day of school was finally over, April stood on the curb in the back of the building waiting for her grandmother to pick her up. She took several steps forward admiring all the nice, clean, parked cars. At first she thought that she must be standing by the teacher's parking lot. But as more students exited the building, she saw them get in the cars and drive off. In her old neighborhood, if a high schooler was lucky enough to drive, it would be an old American clunker or a basic sedan that their parents bought them used or passed down to them like her Grandmother was giving her now that Pastor upgraded her to a Jag. But these spoiled rich kids were driving brand new Mercedes-Benz, Audis, and BMWs. Teenagers with foreign luxury cars. If April didn't know that she was in a different world before, she definitely knew it now.

7

Felicia worshipped the ground her daddy walked on, but he was no saint. He spent many nights at the neighborhood bar and there was talk about him having other women. But he was good to her so that's all that mattered in her mind. He died suddenly one day shortly after her longtime boyfriend and father of her three kids ran off. The combination of losing both of the most important men in her life in such a short period of time drove her over the edge.

All she did at that time in her life was smoke crack to numb her pain. But she had been clean and sober for nearly eight months now. That's what missing a court date, getting arrested, held without a bond, and being forced to go to rehab will do for you. Although she didn't want to go at the time, rehab was one of the best things to ever happen to her. Now that she was off drugs, she wanted to get her kids back from her mother.

She heard through the grapevine that her mother and Pastor Williams were taking their relationship to the next level by getting married. But she had to see for herself how her mother had gone from being the wife of a man who you couldn't get inside a church unless you put a gun to his head, to being the first lady of a very prominent church. So she waited until everyone's attention was on the bride and groom at the front of the church and found a spot on the back pew to slide into. The light was shining right on her mother. She was naturally a pretty woman who didn't like too much makeup. If it took longer than sixty seconds to do it, she couldn't be bothered. But someone else had done a wonderful job applying her makeup. Even her gray hair was shimmering. She looked like a brand-new woman. But more than anything, Felicia noticed how happy her mom looked.

Next, Felicia observed her kids. April looked like a nice young lady with her well-kept haircut. Brooklyn was getting taller, but was still adorable in her purple bridesmaid dress that matched her sister's. Felicia couldn't help the smirk that spread across her face when she noticed Anthony Jr. fussing with his collar and bowtie. It was a big step up from his usual Polo shirts, jeans, and high-top sneakers. She put money on it that as soon as they were finished taking family photos, Jr. would beg to change clothes.

It made her kind of sad not to be included in the pictures on such a big day for her mother. But the last time she had shown her face in this building was when she blackmailed Pastor Zachariah Williams and his son, Assistant Pastor Joshua Williams. Threatening to expose the pastor's son as a child molester had gotten her a check for five thousand dollars before she got kicked out of Joshua's office. Obviously, he had survived her threat because he was the minister marrying her mother and Pastor. Felicia missed her kids terribly, but she didn't feel that barging in on this wedding was the best thing to do. So she snuck out of the church before the end of the joyful ceremony.

Felicia knew that everyone would be shocked to see her again. But it was time. The happy couple should be back from their honeymoon by now. She wasn't going to call anyone to announce she was coming; she planned to show up and get a big welcome from her kids. Well, maybe not April, but Brooklyn and Anthony were always overjoyed to see her. When Felicia pulled up to her old house, there was a for sale sign out on the front lawn. She parked her Chevy and got out to examine the sign. After adding the realtor's number to her contacts, she walked up to the porch intending to knock on the front door. But the chairs that used to be on the porch weren't there. Her mother's curtains were gone too, which allowed her to see into the house to discover the living room furniture had been moved out as well. The house was empty. *I should have known Pastor wouldn't actually live in this neighborhood. It's good enough for his congregation, but not good enough for him I guess.*

She sighed, sat down on the steps and reflected on her childhood. All of the girls on the street used to Double Dutch in front of her house because she lived in the middle of the street. They had time to stop jumping rope and move out of the way before a car reached them from either direction. Felicia was never as good at it as the others, but it was still fun trying. She loved when all of the kids, boys and girls, got together to play kickball. The tree in front of her house was third base. This house even made her think about her kids' father, Anthony Senior. He had snuck out her back door plenty of days before her mother got home from work. All of the memories that came from growing up in this house made her sad realizing that it would soon belong to some other family. She wondered if they would have kids or if it would be a starter home for newlyweds with no children. After taking a deep breath, Felicia slowly walked back to her car and took one last look at her former home before buckling up and pulling away from the curb.

The afternoon hadn't turned out as planned. She envisioned spending the evening reuniting with her kids and even battling with her mother about why she hadn't called in the last nine months. It was going to be difficult to explain to her mom that she didn't want to come back until she had herself together.

Her children had been through a lot in the last few years. Their dad abandoning the family because the police were looking into his drug dealing was just the beginning of her family's downward spiral. It didn't take long for Felicia to turn to the same drug he sold to support their family to relieve her pain. As much as she tried to hide it from her kids, they knew something was going on. They went from being spoiled kids of a drug dealer that got everything they ever thought they wanted, to having a mother who spent every dime she could get her hands on to feed her addiction, leaving them with little or nothing. Then when she got arrested she vowed to get her life together. But she wasn't out a full twenty-four hours without taking advantage of an unexpected opportunity to get some fast money. Even though her heart was telling her not to do it, her brain was telling her this was her chance to kill two birds with one stone. She could get high one last time and have the money to get back on her feet. All she had to do was blackmail the assistant pastor. She wasn't sure if she believed April's accusations against him or not. At the time it didn't matter. All that mattered was the money. But once she started getting high with the money, she couldn't stop herself. The next thing she knew, it was a week later and she and her friends had smoked up five thousand dollars' worth of crack. The money she needed to start over was gone.

Felicia was too ashamed to show her face at her mother's house again. So she stayed with her friend until she got stopped by the police for questioning. Once they ran her name and found out she had a warrant for her arrest for not appearing at a court date, she was arrested again. Luckily, after a couple months, she harped on the fact that she had three kids waiting on her and a sympathetic judge sent her to rehab center instead of back to county jail. Now that she was finally clean and had a job, she wanted her children back with her even if it meant it would make the friction between her and her mother worse.

Today was supposed to be her day off, but she decided that since she couldn't be with her family, she might as well go into work and earn some money. Her boss called her about a half hour ago and asked if she could come in because someone had called in sick, but she declined. Felicia quickly dialed his number and asked if he had found a replacement yet. When her supervisor said he hadn't, she agreed to pick up the shift and told him she would be there as soon as she went home and changed clothes.

Felicia sat in the parking lot of her job taking a few minutes to mentally get herself together. One had to be in the right frame of mind when you stepped through the threshold of this building. She would have liked to stay in her air-conditioned car a little longer, but she noticed a line of cars waiting to pay forming at the parking lot entrance. The spots were filling up fast so she wanted to get inside and start making some money. But the September humidity slapped her in the face as soon as she opened her car door and stepped out. She almost got back in.

As she bypassed the line of men standing to pay the cover charge to enter the club, she could sense them examining her wondering what her body looked like under her outfit. They probably assumed that she was one of the club's strippers, but she wasn't. She was only a waitress. And that was good enough for her. No one would ever mistake her as shy. But she didn't have the courage or the type of mentality that it took to be dancing totally naked in a room full of a hundred men. So although she didn't bring home nearly as much as the dancers did, she made pretty good money in tips serving watered down drinks and some pretty good wings to a bunch of horny men. Some of them figured that she was an aspiring dancer waiting for her turn on the poles on stage. They were constantly propositioning her to do private lap dances for them in their car in the parking lot or to come home with them at the end of the night. Felicia made the mistake of being insulted and cursing out the first couple of guys that made this suggestion to her. They repaid her by not leaving her a gratuity when they paid their tabs. Learning quickly from her error, she became an expert at grinning and bearing it. One of her mother's favorite sayings that she heard growing up was, "You catch more bees with honey than you do with vinegar." So she flirted and let them think they might have a chance until she received her tips and then rejected her admirers as gently as possible.

Working at Club Stiletto wasn't the best job in the world, but after growing up depending on her parents and then Anthony Senior to provide for her all her life, it felt good to be able to financially support herself for once. Hopefully, her holier-than-thou mother would see it the same way.

8

"Hold on." Zachariah stopped talking and glanced at the screen of his Motorola cell phone to see who else was calling him now. He quickly decided that whatever Mary wanted was going to have to wait. "Never mind man. I'm here. I'll call my wife back later." Zachariah sighed heavily. "I can't believe this. When I saw him last month he looked fine."

"I guess he wasn't as healthy as he seemed. They say men don't go to the doctor as much as we should. Maybe he ignored the warning signs," Donald suggested.

Zachariah thought about it and shook his head. "I suppose that's a possibility. Robert did say that he was feeling a little tired. And as hard as he tried to stop, he couldn't stop smoking those nasty cigarettes. But one minute you're fine, the next you are being rushed to the hospital, and then you are dead a few hours later. He was only sixty-five years old. This is unbelievable."

"What can you do? I guess God was ready for him to come home."

He shook his head and gritted his teeth. Pausing for a second to think about what Donald said, Zachariah decided not to comment on it. After all, he had made the very same stupid comment to people in the past. Being on the other side of the situation, right now he realized how insensitive it sounded.

"Well if this traffic ever starts moving again, I'm on my way over there to talk to the family. Hopefully, I can come up with some comforting words."

Donald inquired, "What are you saying? You've helped countless people through tough times in their lives. This isn't your first rodeo Pastor."

Zachariah was quiet for a few more seconds. He tried to find the right words to explain to his assistant pastor that this was different. This was one of his friends from seminary school. As pastors, they led very busy lives and didn't keep in touch as much as they should have and now his friend was gone. And this was the second time someone he was close to passed away this month. Just a few weeks ago, right before the wedding, he got a similar phone call saying one of his old high school buddies was dead. He was only sixty-one. The doctors said his diabetes caused his kidneys to fail. Zachariah tried not to let it affect him too much because it was his wedding week, but now it was happening again.

Was he really at that age where his friends started dropping like flies? It was nice to run into people from time to time at social events and hear about who was finally out of jail, how many grandkids or great-grandkids someone had or who was on marriage number three or four. But were frequent funerals going to become the place where he caught up with his old high school and seminary classmates to find out who was still alive and who had passed away? Is that what he had to look forward to from now on until it was his turn?

"Pastor, are you still there?"

"Yes, I'm here." He tried to sound more together than he really was. "Listen, thanks for letting me know what happened. I'm heading over to Robert's house to check on his wife. I'll see you tomorrow at the church." Zachariah hung up before Donald could give him any more bad news.

As he drove in evening rush hour traffic on I-285, he reminisced about his friend and all the good times that they had together. They used to go on double dates before they married their wives. This was before either of them had any money so they had to scrape together as much as they could to have cheap dates. Luckily, both of their girls really loved them. Later, they were each other's groomsmen at their weddings. Zachariah selected Robert as Joshua and David's Godfather without any reservations. And he was his kid's Godfather in return. Both families even went on vacations together to Disney World in Florida and Myrtle Beach in South Carolina when their kids were little. They were still the best of friends, but as both of their churches flourished and their kids grew up, their families didn't hang out as much as they used to. Robert showed that he was still a loyal friend by coming around checking on him when Gloria was sick and kept doing so after she passed away. But you can't go on double dates with your friend and his wife anymore when your spouse is gone. Now that Zachariah was remarried, he would never get the chance to take Mary on any double dates with the Thompsons.

Zachariah thought back to August and realized that the final time he saw his buddy was at the wedding and reception. He reasoned that if something was wrong with Robert then, he was too busy celebrating his nuptials with Mary to notice it and he felt so bad about that. Thinking about his recent wedding day made him remember that he had ignored his wife's call. So he picked his phone back up and dialed home.

Mary picked up on the first ring and immediately started fussing. "Baby I just tried to call you. Why didn't you answer?"

"Hey sweetheart. I know." Zachariah sighed. "I just found out that Pastor Thompson died last night."

"What? Oh no. Baby, I'm so sorry. We just saw him."

"I know. That's the same thing I said. His wife called the church right after I left to come home. Donald took the call and called me. So I'm on my way over to their house now to see what I can do to help the family make the funeral arrangements."

"Okay. Tell her that I'll be praying for them. And I will see you when you get home. I love you."

That was the best thing he had heard all day so it brought a big smile to his face. "I love you too. See you later, baby."

After a couple hours of trying to comfort the bereaved family and reading scriptures, Zachariah felt drained. Normally, quoting the word would not only make others feel good, but it would uplift him as well. But not tonight. He had done his job and blessed the family with words of encouragement, but he still felt horrible. And the person that he would call in a situation like this for reassurance because he could relate to what he was going through, was laying on a slab at the morgue waiting to be picked up by the funeral home. Zachariah had to leave. It was too painful to stay in his friend's house any longer without him being there. But he wasn't ready to go home yet.

Before Zachariah realized what he was doing, he found himself pulling into the parking lot of Applebee's just a few minutes from home. He loved their ribs, but that wasn't what he was in the mood for right now. Besides, while he was at his friend's home, there was a steady stream of family and close friends dropping by with Tupperware containers and casserole dishes full of good smelling food. He also knew that Mary probably had a plate of delicious food covered and piled high sitting in the microwave ready to heat up for him the minute he arrived home. But even though he had skipped lunch, he hadn't had an appetite since he received the devastating news.

Zachariah walked in the entryway and waited for the hostess to return to the podium. He searched the restaurant as far as his eyes could see for any familiar faces. He wasn't near his church, but he had members from all over town. Brows would be raised if any of them saw him out drinking. But he didn't feel like sitting in a secluded booth by himself so he took his chances and seated himself directly at the bar anyway. The U-shaped bar had several other groups of young guys seated watching a Braves game on the TV. He skipped a seat and sat down near a man that looked close to his age that was drinking alone. They exchanged a nod of the head as he settled on the barstool. The bartender quickly approached and put a drink napkin down. Zachariah paused and stared at the napkin for a few seconds. The bartender clearing his throat grabbed his attention. He stopped hesitating and ordered a rum and coke and an order of baby back ribs with fries just in case he saw someone he knew. Zachariah figured it might even be a good idea for him to try and eat some of it so Mary wouldn't smell the rum he was about to consume.

His plan was to have one stiff drink to calm his nerves before heading home. The news he received today unsettled him and he needed to regroup somehow. But four drinks later he was still sitting at the bar sipping and enjoying the conversation with the man next to him. His new buddy's name was Walter. He was divorced and lived nearby so he was a regular there. Instead of sitting at home alone consuming bad TV dinners, Walter came here most nights to eat and watch whatever sporting event was on TV. Zachariah remembered his brief time living alone after his wife died. Without any warning, the house he loved seemed too big for only him. And it was extremely quiet and lonely. So he could understand Walter longing to be surrounded by noisy people, even if they were strangers.

Zachariah's phone rang interrupting their conversation. Mary's name popped up, but what caught his attention was the time that showed up at the top of the screen. It was nearly midnight. He answered but intended to make this a short conversation. "Hey. I'm sorry that it took longer than I expected, but I'm on my way home right now."

"Is that music that I hear in the background? Where are you baby? It doesn't sound like you are still at the Thompson's house."

Zachariah's eyes darted around. He had been inside so long that he didn't realize how noisy it was with people laughing, the music playing, and the loud television the bartender turned up for Walter. He wasn't about to confess that he desperately needed a drink to his wife though. So he dodged her questions. "I just had to make a quick stop, but I'm on my way home. Bye baby." He pushed the red phone button to hang up on her before she had the opportunity to ask anything else.

"Alright man. I gotta get home to my wife and grandkids." Zachariah commented as he pulled his credit card out to pay his bill. When his tab was paid, he stood up to leave and extended his hand to Walter. "It was nice meeting you man."

"You too. See you around," Walter said as he shook his hand and then pulled out his card to head out as well.

9

It was the morning of Pastor Robert Thompson's services. Funerals were routine occurrences in Zachariah's line of work. They never used to bother him. That is until his wife Gloria died. Prior to her death, he saw them as a necessary part of the circle of life. Showing up, he sincerely helped the family in any way he could, but went through the motions unfazed. But now each funeral was a reminder that he had lost the love of his life. He felt as helpless as a baby during her bout with cancer. Praying and bargaining with the Lord had not been successful. She never recovered. They were supposed to grow old together and take care of each other. But it didn't work out like they planned.

The older he got, the more funerals he had to attend. It was like someone kept constantly picking at his wound preventing it from fully healing. Today, he woke up not only remembering the life of his dear friends, but mourning the loss of his first wife all over again. He reached in his dresser drawer and pulled out the picture of her. Although his spirit was low, the sight of her lovely round face brought a momentary smile to his lips, but it didn't last. Zachariah stood there staring at her faded picture for a few minutes until he couldn't take it anymore. Putting the picture back in the drawer under his stack of undershirts, he closed his eyes.

He tried to talk himself out of what he was about to do next, but he couldn't think of a good enough reason not to do it. Zachariah needed to do this and then he would feel better and now was the perfect opportunity to do so. Mary was busy in their bathroom getting ready to go with him and if any of the kids were awake, they hadn't made their way downstairs yet. So he slid on his house shoes, grabbed the keys to his Benz holding them tight so they wouldn't make any noise, and made his way to the garage. Pulling the door open, Zachariah closed it behind him as slowly and quietly as possible. Once he was seated in his vehicle, he opened his glove compartment. A few seconds later, the little black flask was in his hand and up to his mouth. How was it possible that the gulp of straight rum he swallowed, simultaneously burned his throat, calmed his nerves, and empowered him to face the day's activities at the same time? Sitting in the garage lit by the interior car light and the rising morning sunlight, he remained there until the container was empty, only getting out when he thought he heard a noise coming from inside the house. If someone was in the kitchen now, he was going to have to explain what he was doing out in the garage. So before he went back in the house, he hastily swished some mouthwash around in his mouth before discreetly spitting it in the garage trash can.

Mary turned from the refrigerator and looked at her husband up and down with a smile on her face. "Hey. What were you doing out in the garage, baby?"

"I thought I left my cell phone in the car," he answered quickly, diverting his eyes.

She shook her head and giggled. "Your phone is in there on your nightstand," she replied pointing towards their bedroom like he was an absentminded old man.

"Okay. Thanks." Zachariah turned and walked away.

He knew full well where his cell phone was, but that was the best excuse he came up with. Lying to his wife was not something that he liked to do, but it was better than defending why he had been out in the garage drinking alcohol. It was too early in the morning for her judgmental words. He felt bad enough as it was that he couldn't hold it together today. Besides, her friends weren't dying every month like his were so she couldn't possibly understand.

As much as he hated to admit it, these turn of events had really shaken him. They had him thinking about his own mortality. And he wasn't ready to face thoughts of his demise yet. He still had things that he wanted to do if only the people in his life would cooperate. He couldn't even retire early like he thought he would be able to do by now because last year Joshua dropped the bombshell that he didn't want to take over Mt. Zion as head pastor. Then he inherited a ready-made house full of grandkids when he married Mary. He had the expenses of a new house, new furniture, tuition for three kids, and a wife that he was beginning to realize was buying whatever she wanted without looking at the price tag for the first time in her life. At the rate things were going, Mary and those three would have him in the poor house. He had to keep working hard because they kept spending.

Later that day, Zachariah paid his respects to his friend by being among the ministers that said a few words at his wake. First Lady Thompson had also asked him and several other ministers to be pallbearers. Of course he didn't want to turn the widow down, but he had mixed feelings about carrying another buddy to his final resting place. It was hard enough watching women and children cry, but several grown men including Robert's sons openly wept when people spoke about how he had served God well with his work. The sounds began to disturb Zachariah. Not caring how it looked, he got up during the service and went outside the church to get some fresh air. Mary attempted to grab his hand when he stood up, but he shook her loose so that he could be alone. A few minutes later, Mary stuck her head out the door looking for him. *Can't she tell that I need a minute?*

"Baby, are you alright?"

That was a stupid question and he almost told her as much. Instead he huffed, but remained silent.

"The service is almost over, baby. It's time for you to come back inside if you are going to be one of the pallbearers."

"Okay. I'll be right in," he calmly answered and stared at Mary indicating that she could go back inside without him. He wasn't angry with his wife. Keeping his distance from her made it easier because he was already planning to break away from this group of pastors, pastor's wives, church folks, and mourners the first chance he got. Tonight, he needed to be with people full of life. His spirit couldn't handle any more sorrow today. She gazed back at him and her mouth opened slightly like she was considering insisting that he come with her. But without any resistance, she suddenly retreated, marching across the lobby and back into the wake. Not wanting to hold up the service, Zachariah went back inside shortly behind her.

Along with the other pastors, he carried the casket to the hearse and then out again for the burial. He was tired of giving eulogies, comforting relatives, and being a pallbearer. All of it was draining his spirit. Right now, Zachariah felt like he had two strikes against him. He was a man and a minister. When boys are young they are told not to cry. Man up. No one ever teaches them what to do with their emotions. And as a minister no one thinks to ask how you are doing because it's your job to encourage everyone else. If you tell someone how you truly feel they don't know what to say and will lose confidence in you as a spiritual leader. So he stood quietly near his friend's casket and anxiously waited for this day to be over with.

Next, everyone gathered at the repast at the Thompson's house. Their house was large, but it seemed small because each room was packed with family and members from the Thompson's church, there to pay their respects. The four burners on the kitchen stove and the countertops were loaded with food that the family had prepared and others brought to help meet the burden of feeding a houseful of mourners. Once everyone got food in their bellies they began to be more upbeat. But Zachariah barely touched the plate of food that his wife fixed for him. Any other time he would have devoured it, but he didn't have an appetite for food. He was eager to leave. The only thing stopping him was that he didn't want the awkward feeling of being the first person to hug First Lady Thompson and explain why he had to leave so soon.

Everyone else sat around laughing and remembering their minister and dear friend. Zachariah noticed a few of the saints drinking wine. So he slowly eased over to the bar. There were several new bottles of red and white wines. Zachariah suspected that they were purchased for today, but he needed something a little stronger. A light layer of dust on the random gin and vodka bottles spoke to the fact that his friends were not big drinkers. Finally, he found an almost full bottle of rum. It wasn't his top shelf brand but it would do. After pouring some in his cup, he walked to the refrigerator and retrieved a can of Coke to mix it with. Zachariah chose to only use a little of the Coke making sure that his drink was stiff. As soon as he took his first sip, he felt his wife eyeing him from across the dining room. It must be driving her crazy to see him boldly drinking out in public. Zachariah's cheeks inflated as he took a big gulp and all but dared her to say anything to him. After all, he was a grown man. She looked to her left and to her right probably trying to see if anyone was paying attention to him sitting there next to the bar. But he realized that no one was. Mary turned to leave the room and Zachariah took another big swallow that burned his throat before filling up his cup again.

It wasn't long before Zachariah felt the mood altering effects of his drinks. He eventually joined in the loud conversations and even shared some funny stories of his own about his good friend. Mary politely tapped him on his shoulder and asked, "Are you ready to leave?" The anxious look on her face let him know that he had managed to say or do something to embarrass her. He didn't know why she was being so uptight. None of these people even attended Mt. Zion. Not ready to leave the gathering that he was finally having fun at, he told her, "Not yet." Then he got up to refill his glass again.

10

Today, Mary was treating her good friend to a trip to the mall. Her book club member Brenda was turning fifty-five and Mary intended to take her to lunch, buy her something nice that she picks out herself, and maybe even get her eyebrows arched if her friend agreed to it. Brenda had the wildest eyebrows Mary had ever seen. Since Mary had been able to afford to get her hair, nails, and eyebrows done on a regular basis now, she hoped that she would be able to convince her friend what she had been missing.

Mary had been so busy the last couple months getting settled in her new home as well as her new role as first lady that she hadn't seen her friend since the wedding. But that was going to change this afternoon and Brenda's birthday was the perfect excuse to make it happen. Mary wanted to pick her up in her Jag and drive her to Phipps Plaza in style, but Brenda insisted she had errands to run and would meet her there at noon.

Impatiently checking her designer watch every few minutes, Mary glanced at the window display of the lingerie store in front of her. If her husband wasn't acting the way he had been carrying on lately, she would gladly buy a new set of bra and panties or even some tasteful intimate apparel to wear for him. But he had been coming home smelling like alcohol was oozing out of his pores, which was a big turn off and reminded her of her first husband. So she quickly removed the lingerie idea from her head.

Brenda was ten minutes late so far. They agreed to meet at the mall entrance to Saks Fifth Avenue. That worked out fine with what Mary planned. She would walk her friend up one level and persuade her to get her eyebrows done. If she didn't see anything that she wanted as they walked the mall, Mary would take her into her new favorite store, Lord & Taylor. Brenda would definitely find something nice in there before Mary treated her to a delicious lunch.

"Hey. I'm sorry I'm late. The bus took a long time picking us up," Brenda said as she walked up behind Mary slightly out of breath.

"You caught the bus up here?"

"My car is in the shop, so I caught the train to the

station down the street and then the bus dropped me off at the corner. It was either that or have one of those dirty old men in my building bring me. And you know I wasn't doing that. They expect to come into your apartment and get their thank you, if you know what I mean. And that's for taking you down the street to the store. I can only imagine what they would expect you to do for driving you across town." She exhaled and said, "But I guess there's no point in complaining. I'm here now."

Mary shook her head and stared at her buddy. "I don't understand why you wouldn't let me pick you up."

Brenda snapped, "Don't start. I may not have a Jag, but I get around just fine. I don't need you picking me up."

Mary dropped the conversation because she didn't want to argue with Brenda on her birthday. But she didn't understand where that comment came from. She fumbled in her purse for a tissue to wipe her forehead. No matter what food the magazines suggested or supplements she tried she couldn't get rid of the hot flashes that came with menopause. When she found it and looked up, Brenda looked as if she had caught her breath. "Is that a new bag?"

Mary quickly looked back down to see which purse she was carrying. "Yes, I just got this Louis Vuitton last week." Mary held it out and turned it around so Brenda could get a good look at it. "Do you like it?"

"Sure," Brenda said, looking straight ahead. "How much did it cost?"

"I don't remember. Around a thousand I think."

Brenda sucked her teeth and mumbled, "Hmm. Must be nice."

Rolling her eyes and switching the subject Mary said, "Oh. Happy birthday. I want you to pick out something and I'll get it as my present to you."

Brenda raised her eyebrow and Mary could tell she was fighting to hold back a smile. *I knew that would change her attitude.*

"Well let's see if I can find something on sale," Brenda said and turned towards the department store.

"Okay. We have a one thirty lunch reservation though so let's get moving. And if you can't find anything in here, there is always Lord & Taylor."

Brenda started laughing. "Since when did you start shopping in these overpriced stores?"

"Recently. And they aren't as high as you probably think." Mary said as she waved her hand. "Besides, it's your birthday. Please let me do something special for you."

Brenda shrugged her shoulders and rolled her eyes. "Okay. It's your money to waste I guess. But I'll try to find something on the clearance rack that won't cost us an arm or a leg."

Thirty minutes later, one of Mary's missions was accomplished. She bought her friend a beautiful silk blouse to wear to her church and got herself a new dress for Sunday morning. It was time to walk her past the eyebrow salon and try to talk her into getting them done. It wasn't easy, but Mary was able to convince Brenda to sit in the chair. But as soon as the lady started doing her brows she screamed. Mary's mouth dropped open. Brenda turned to her and yelled, "I thought you said this wasn't going to hurt?"

"I get it done all the time. It doesn't hurt me." Mary stared at her friend as she held her hand over her right eye and brow. She stopped looking at Mary and was now glaring at the Asian woman standing in front of her with the tweezers in her hand.

Finally, the woman said, "If you don't let me finish you are going to look weird with one brow done and the other one not done." Brenda reluctantly gave in. The way she was gripping the arms of the chair like she was getting a root canal was ridiculous, but at least she wasn't screaming anymore. Mary looked around and the other clients in the store tried to act like they weren't the center of attention. Feeling extremely embarrassed by her friend's behavior, Mary went in her purse and pulled out her American Express credit card to pay so they could leave as quickly as possible.

The entire walk to the restaurant, Brenda complained about her brows burning. Mary was trying to do a good thing and show her friend something new and it had backfired. Instead of her being impressed and happy, her buddy was in a bad mood and trying to get out of going to eat. "I feel a migraine coming on. Maybe we should go to lunch some other time."

"I don't want this to end on a bad note. Once we sit down and eat, your mind won't be on your face anymore." Mary could see Brenda deciding so she kept pushing. "Come on. They have the best eggplant risotto." Suddenly her bestie made a face like she ate something nasty. Maybe she didn't choose the best dish to pique her interest. But Mary didn't let that deter her. She grabbed Brenda by the arm and gently pulled her along.

They arrived at the restaurant a few minutes early so they had to wait for their table. Brenda excused herself to go to the bathroom while Mary waited by the door. "Mary Williams is that you?" Mary turned around and saw Shirley Ward, first lady of New Bethel Baptist Church with two hands full of shopping bags. Even in a casual sweater and jeans, she looked elegant with flawless makeup and bouncy hair that always looked like she just stepped out of the salon. She was the wife of one of Zachariah's acquaintances. Atlanta was a big city yet it was a small world. Most of the Black ministers in town knew each other. The Wards were the well-respected first family of New Bethel.

She put down her bags and the ladies hugged. "Hi. Good to see you again. Zachariah has been telling me that I need to call you. He says that you are a great first lady and that I could learn a lot from you."

Shirley gushed, "Zachariah is so sweet. Yes, my husband has been a pastor for thirty years and I've been right by his side the entire time. You can ask me just about anything."

"So are you here by yourself?" Mary asked.

"Yes. I just ran in to buy a few things," she picked up her bags for emphasis.

Mary looked at all of her bags in amazement and wondered how much damage she could do if she were here all day. Zachariah would hit the roof if she came in with her hands loaded with bags like that. She would have to hide them in the trunk of her car and sneak them in the house one by one over a period of a few days.

"I was walking by on my way to my car and I saw you standing here alone so I figured I would join you."

Right on cue, Brenda returned interrupting their conversation. "Mary, I think I need to go home." Suddenly Mary saw how puffy Brenda's eyebrows were and jerked her head back. They didn't look like that a few minutes ago. She wondered if she had been picking at them in the bathroom mirror just to have an excuse to cut their outing short. "I think I am having a bad reaction to the tweezers."

"Oh sweetheart what happened?" Shirley asked and touched Brenda's shoulder.

Mary introduced the women to each other and then briefly explained the situation to Shirley leaving out the details about Brenda's bad attitude. "I'm so glad that you stopped to talk to me, but I need to get her home."

"No. No. No. You stay and enjoy that eggplant thing you were talking about." Brenda insisted that she could get herself home. Mary had mixed feelings. On one hand she wanted to do the right thing and drive Brenda home since she was upset and took public transportation to meet her. But on the other hand, this was a great opportunity to pick First Lady Ward's brain about her experience being the wife of a head pastor. She really wanted to get to know Shirley, so she hesitantly let her friend have her way for the first time today. Brenda hugged Mary, told Shirley it was nice meeting her, and quickly walked out towards the mall exit without looking back and Mary didn't try to stop her.

Mary watched her friend walk away. It seemed like more was going on than just her going home because she didn't feel well. She felt like Brenda was intentionally pulling away from her for some reason. But she didn't want to tear up in public, especially not in front of Shirley. So she put her feelings aside, determined to have a great lunch and have a come to Jesus talk with her friend later.

11

"Williams, party of two." Mary and Shirley turned toward the hostess and stepped closer. "Right this way ladies." They followed her to a group of tables near the large windows just in time for her to see Brenda walking across the parking lot. Mary paused, tempted to run out on the patio and tell her friend to wait, that she had changed her mind and was taking her home no matter what she said. But when Shirley touched her arm and asked her what was wrong, she continued following the hostess. "Is this table okay ladies?"

Mary peered out the window to make sure her book club member was truly out of eyesight. "Yes, this is fine. Thank you." She sat down and tried to ignore the puzzled look on Shirley's face. Their waiter promptly saved the day by introducing himself and asking for their drink orders.

Mary ordered water with lemon while Shirley requested a sweet tea.

"Your friend didn't leave because of me, did she?"

Exhaling, Mary decided to be totally transparent with the woman she respected and hoped would turn out to be a new friend. "Honestly I don't know why she left. We've been friends for twenty years, but since Zachariah and I got married she has been distant. I tried to treat her to lunch and pamper her a little for her birthday, but I don't know what went wrong. She has been snapping at me for no reason since we got here."

"Is she married?"

"No. She's never been married."

Shirley glanced down at the lunch menu left by the waiter. "Is she well off or is she struggling financially?"

"Um." The questions being thrown at her surprised Mary a bit. "She struggles a little like most people I guess. But she is fine. She has an apartment in a high rise that she really likes living in."

Shirley nodded her head, but didn't respond. She kept her eyes on the menu. "I think I might treat myself to the filet mignon today."

Mary quickly responded, "Oh no, it's my treat. I wouldn't even still be here if you hadn't said hello to me. I would be on my way home wondering what happened to the nice outing I planned."

Looking up from the menu, Shirley gently asked, "Has it ever crossed your mind that your friend might be a tiny bit jealous of you now that you have a husband and a new house?"

"But this is my second marriage. You probably don't know this, but I was married before. My first husband died."

"You're right. I didn't know. I'm sorry to hear that."

"She didn't act like this when I was married before. So I don't think it's that."

"Well let me ask you this. Was your first husband as rich and handsome as Pastor Williams?"

The way Shirley was staring directly at her was making Mary a little uncomfortable. She wanted this woman as a friend, but didn't expect to be getting drilled with tough questions. Mary wanted to be the one asking her questions about being a first lady. The waiter rested their glasses on the table and asked if they were ready to order yet. Mary didn't have a chance to peruse the menu, but there was no need since she had been looking forward to the eggplant risotto all week. As Shirley ordered first, a quick glance at the menu told Mary that the filet mignon cost twenty-eight dollars. Mary had to take a sip of her water to keep from choking. Even though it was her husband's money, this lunch was going to be a lot pricier than she expected. "And for you, ma'am?" Mary ordered her meal, the waiter took their menus, and left the table.

Mary looked at a couple holding hands walking by and smiled.

"Aren't you going to answer my question?" She had almost forgotten, but obviously her lunch date hadn't.

"Yes and no. My first husband was fine, but no he wasn't as rich as Zachariah."

"Well then there you have it." Shirley paused to take a sip of her tea. Mary couldn't help but notice several diamond rings on her fingers and the diamond tennis bracelets that dangled from her wrist. "Your first marriage wasn't a threat to her because you weren't rich. Now you are and she is jealous." Mary threw her hand up in the air and shook her head. Shirley put up her finger to stop her from responding. "Wait a minute. Wait a minute. Hear me out. Before you get upset and tell me I don't know what I'm talking about, I've seen it happen a million times." She moved her hand to her chest and announced, "It's happened to me before."

Mary finally interrupted the first lady to set her straight. "Number one, I'm not rich. And my friend isn't like that."

Shrugging her shoulders Shirley appeared to give up. A few seconds later, she started talking again. "My hubby told me about the Jaguar you got as a wedding present." Mary couldn't help the grin that came to her lips. Shirley continued, "Was she excited about you having a new Jag?" And just like that her smile faded. Come to think of it, Mary didn't remember Brenda being happy for her, but she was not going to give Shirley that satisfaction. That didn't stop her persistent lunch companion though. "What about your new house? Has she been there yet?" Mary recalled inviting Brenda over and her cancelling at the last minute by saying she didn't feel well. Shirley interrupted her train of thought by asking, "Does she ever attend the church that you are now first lady of?"

This was getting ridiculous now. Everything she was saying may very well be true, but surely the woman sitting directly across the table from her could see how uncomfortable she was making her feel. Perhaps Shirley wasn't as classy as Mary thought she was. Mary unrolled the silverware from her napkin and placed it on her lap. She took a sip of her water in an attempt to control her temper. Zachariah wouldn't want her to curse out another pastor's wife, but that is exactly what was going to happen if Ms. Know-It-All didn't back off.

"I'm sorry Mary. I didn't mean to be so presumptuous. But sometimes you can't bring everyone with you."

Mary wanted to insist that she was wrong again, but she couldn't because she was slowly realizing that everything she said was right. So she settled on, "It's okay. I can see how it might look that way to an outsider."

During lunch, their conversation lightened up for a while. Shirley told Mary about her involvement in the women's ministry at her church. Then she went on and on about a recent vacation to Hawaii with her husband. How much fun they had visiting the different islands. On their last night, they went to a big luau with delicious food, fire dancers and learned to hula. Then she winked and asked, "So how was the honeymoon?"

Mary couldn't help but laugh. "It was fun for a few days until we got a call about the bathroom and hallway of Mt. Zion flooding and my new husband left me alone to come back home to handle it." Even the woman who claimed she'd seen and heard it all as a pastor's wife seemed shocked.

"Did you say he left you alone in Jamaica on your honeymoon?" Mary shook her head. "Well I certainly hope you ran his credit card all the way up to the limit for that."

"Believe me, I tried." The two women enjoyed a good laugh about it.

Shirley stopped laughing long enough to say, "What good is a husband if you can't spend his money, right?"

"But seriously. I was really hurt by that," Mary confessed.

"I know you were. It's crazy that he would do that on your honeymoon. But honestly, it won't be the last time that the church takes priority over you, so you might as well get used to it."

Shirley stared at Mary as she put her hand up to her forehead at the thought of what she said. "Listen. You've got it easy."

Mary looked at her wondering what in the world

she was talking about. "When I married my husband, he had dreams of having his own church. So he left the church where we were and opened a storefront church. For six months it was only him, me, and about ten other people. I was really discouraged. I wanted his dream to come true and I was scared that it wouldn't. But he never gave up. No matter how rough it got. There were times when he had two other jobs so he was never home. I was clipping coupons and buying our clothes and furniture from Goodwill. Slowly but surely word got out about our little church and more people started coming. After a few years we were able to move to a bigger space. It was rough in the beginning, but look at us now."

"Wow. You really have come a long way together."

"Yes we have. My point is, you get to reap all the benefits without any of the struggle."

Mary didn't appreciate Shirley's assumptions or like the direction this conversation was headed again and she was going to put a stop to it right now. She was a Grady baby from southwest Atlanta better known as the S.W.A.T.S. So she knew how to handle herself when she had to, but this conversation required some tact. Clearly, Shirley didn't know who she was messing with, but she was about to find out. The new first lady stared directly in the other first lady's face and said, "Well maybe you don't know it, but I've been a member of Mt. Zion since the beginning thirty years ago when it was only about a hundred of us. So I wasn't his wife, but I've been around. I've paid my tithes, volunteered in just about every ministry there is and up until recently I was on the usher board. I still help my husband out every week in the church office like I did before I was his wife. So you see, I put a lot of sweat equity in this church long before I was first lady, but I would love my husband even if it was still only one hundred of us."

Shirley sat back and smirked. "Well, I'm impressed. I didn't know any of that." She put her hands up in mock surrender. "Point taken. Then you truly have earned your spot as first lady. My mistake."

Mary would be glad when this disastrous lunch was over with.

12

"Mt. Zion Baptist Church. Mary speaking. How can I help you?"

"Hello. I see you're still answering the phone for Pastor."

Mary held the phone for a few seconds before responding. It had been a long time since she heard the voice on the other end, but she would recognize it any day. She snapped out of it and with a bit of an attitude responded, "Do you have a problem with that?"

"No ma'am, I don't." Mary didn't hear anything for a few seconds. "I went by the house and saw the for sale sign."

"And?"

Mary could hear the hesitation in her daughter's voice as she said, "I didn't realize that you and the kids had moved."

"If you hadn't disappeared once you got your hands on some of Zachariah's money last year, you would have known," Mary snapped back, not giving her a break. Their conversation had started out wrong and was getting worse by the second. "Look, what do you want? Zachariah is not giving you any more money. So if that's why you called, you are wasting your time."

"I didn't call for any money, Ma. I called because I want to see my kids."

"Hmph. What makes you think they want to see you?" Even Mary knew that was hitting below the belt when Felicia didn't have a quick comeback. But it didn't stop her. She exhaled and confessed, "I never thought that any child of mine could stay away from her kids so long without even so much as a collect phone call. And now you just want to pop back up in their lives with no explanation? Where have you been, Felicia?" Even though she didn't curse, Mary's blood was boiling and she wished that she wasn't sitting in the house of the Lord so she could let loose a couple four letter words on her only child.

Felicia let out a heavy sigh and explained, "I was in jail, Ma. Since I took Pastor's money, I was too embarrassed to call you when I got locked up again. But I'm out now. I'm clean and I even have a job." She began to work herself up to yelling. "And I want to see my kids whether they want to see me or not. But I don't believe you. I know my babies miss me just as much as I miss them."

Her voice was raised too high to be talking to the woman taking care of her three kids in Mary's opinion. She hadn't heard from her in months and here she was calling and being disrespectful. Mary exhaled, not quite knowing how to respond. But then she quickly remembered how Zachariah was always using her or the kids as a way out when he dealt with pushy salesmen or members of the congregation that put him on the spot. She replied in a professional tone as if she were handling Mt. Zion business when the church custodian walked by. "Let me talk to my husband and the kids to see how they feel first. What number can I call you back on?"

Still yelling, Felicia demanded, "Wait a minute. Are you serious? I don't understand why you have to get permission from him so I can see my kids. They are MY kids, not his."

Mary lowered her voice and threatened, "You'd better stop hollering at me or the next thing you hear will be a dial tone. Since he has been taking care of YOUR kids since we got married, I want to talk to him and if you have a problem with that too bad. You should have thought about that before you abandoned your children."

"I didn't abandon them. I just left them with their grandmother for a while so I could get myself together. Now that I am clean, I'm ready to see them. No matter what you say, you can't tell me that my kids don't love and miss me."

Mary didn't want to continue arguing with Felicia. And she didn't want the custodian to overhear her yelling so she ended their conversation as quickly as she could. "Are you going to give me a number to call you back on or not?" She jotted down the number Felicia gave, told her she would call her back, and hung up without saying goodbye.

She knew that one day Felicia would come back for her kids, but the more time passed, the further it slipped to the back of her mind. The day had finally arrived, right when they were settled into their new life and Mary was totally unprepared. She loved her grandbabies and had no intention of disrupting their lives by sending them back to their mother. Mary remembered the way their apartment looked the day she rescued them from that hellhole when Felicia got arrested the first time. The sink was full of caked on dirty dishes, trash bags were overflowing and stinking up the apartment, the dirty laundry in the clothes hamper was taller than she was, and roaches roamed freely without fear of being squished. The kids were a mess as well. They all had on dirty clothes. April hadn't had a relaxer put in her hair in months. Brooklyn's braids were loose and standing on top of her head. And Anthony smelled like sewage. Mary wasn't going to take the chance and subject them to that way of life with their mother again.

With her and Zachariah, they lived in a nice spacious clean house in a safe neighborhood, went to a prestigious private school, ate delicious home cooked meals every night, were well groomed, and most importantly were loved and supervised. Their lifestyle had improved significantly. Anyone could see that. Maybe once Felicia saw how well her kids were doing she would let them stay. Mary replayed her conversation with her daughter. *Did she say she wanted to get her kids? No, she hadn't. She said she wanted to see her kids.* Maybe Mary was jumping the gun. Hopefully she was worrying for nothing.

Getting up from her desk, she marched the few steps into her husband's office to tell him what just happened. "Felicia just called." To her surprise Zachariah's eyebrows raised, quickly followed up by the smile that formed on his lips. He seemed happy that Felicia was back in their lives. After all the pain that Felicia had put both of their families through, Mary couldn't understand his cheerful reaction. Why wasn't he upset like she was? "What are you grinning for?"

"Calm down baby. It was a natural reaction to smile. When she first disappeared you called the hospital and the morgue praying that nothing horrible happened to her." He turned her question back around to her. "Why aren't you happy that she is okay?"

Mary folded her arms, refusing to respond and admit that her husband had made his point. She was a bit relieved that her daughter was okay.

Zachariah asked, "What did she say Mary?"

"She said that she had been in jail, but now she is out. That she is clean, employed, and wants to see the kids."

"Mary, if Felicia is off drugs like she says she is then she should be allowed to see her kids. Brooklyn and Anthony haven't mentioned her lately, but you know that they will want to see her." He shrugged his shoulders and continued, "I don't know about April, but she needs to spend some time with her mother as well." Then he got up from his desk and moved closer. "Remember that you must forgive others if you want God to forgive you."

With that being said, Mary narrowed her eyes and exhaled. There was no point in trying to sway her husband over to her way of thinking. She knew his mind was already made up so their conversation was over. She also was conscious of the fact that her husband had a lot on his mind since he had just lost another close friend. So she reluctantly dropped the subject of her wayward child for now.

13

April was surprised when a White girl, who usually didn't talk to her, came to her cafeteria table and invited her to a party at her house that weekend. Then she showed her true intentions by asking April to score some crack and they would reimburse her when she got there. Rolling her eyes, April declined the invite to the party. The girl walked away returning to her lunch table. She shook her head and the entire table either put their heads down, shook their head, threw their hands up in the air or pounded on the table.

April turned and looked at Robin in shock. "Did she only invite me because they thought since I was Black that

I had the hookup on getting drugs?"

"Yep. I think so." She looked at April's expression and commented, "Forget them. They are a bunch of idiots."

"I didn't want to go to her stupid party anyway. But I don't like the fact that she just tried to play me for a fool."

April imagined what was happening on the other side of town with her old classmates. She couldn't wait until they got a week off for Thanksgiving break soon so she could get away from these kids. As usual, Robin was talking her head off, but April had learned how to tune her out weeks ago. Robin was actually beginning to grow on her. Despite her unrelenting gift of gab, she was pretty cool for a White girl. April came to the conclusion that Robin was tired of being a loner and had attached herself to the new Black girl, figuring that they could be outcasts together.

Little did Robin know that April never intended to try and fit in with this crowd. It seemed like they were trying to fit into what came natural to her more than the other way around. There were plenty of times she heard Summertime by Will Smith blasting in a passing car and expected to see a Black person, but it was a blond-haired blue-eyed White boy bobbing his head in the driver's seat. The girls at her school loved Yo-Yo and MC Lyte. And the boys hung out around their cars after school trying to be as cool as the Boyz n the Hood. But from the way most of them shunned her, April figured out that loving Black culture and loving Black people were two entirely different things.

And when the crowd wasn't trying to be hip, they talked about regular trips with their families to places like London and Paris. Places April never even thought about going. Some of them were upset that they had to spend their summers working entry-level jobs at the companies their parents ran instead of automatically working alongside them. They had allowances, nice cars, vacation homes, and jobs waiting for them when they graduated, yet they idolized songs about getting money by hustling in the streets. But in reality, most of them wouldn't last five minutes in April's old neighborhood without wetting their pants.

It wasn't always cool living in the hood. When you are a little kid trying to go to sleep, but a group of young guys are hanging outside laughing and blasting music in their cars. Everyone was too scared to say anything to them, because they probably had guns on them and wouldn't hesitate to shoot anyone trying to punk them in front of their boys. When they lived in the apartment complex, if their neighbor had rats and roaches, that meant you did too regardless of how clean you kept your place. And if you lived in a home, it wasn't uncommon to see abandoned house after abandoned house as you were walking down your street. If these rich kids knew what April knew, they wouldn't be complaining about their sheltered pampered lives.

The first week that April was there, one of the girls called her ghetto because she was popping her gum in the cafeteria. It took all of her willpower not to show the unsuspecting girl just how ghetto she really was by beating her unconscious. As much as she didn't like that school, she knew that Pastor was paying a lot of money for her to attend and her grandmother would be livid if she got kicked out. So she controlled her temper. Her therapist would be proud of her for that. Even though she knew that she didn't want to fight, April made it a point to move into the girl's personal space and put her finger in her face so she knew April could do something to her if she chose to. The girl blinked and backed up a little. Apparently, she came to her senses and recognized that April was not to be messed with.

But April was not the kind of girl who chose to fight all the time anymore. Last year, she was suspended from school for everything from fighting to getting caught having sex in a classroom after school. April's doctor helped her see that she was bringing all the bad things that were going on at home with her to school. She didn't have any control over her father leaving the house and never returning. And she didn't have the power to make her mom stop getting high to numb her pain. So with no parental supervision, she found herself taking care of her younger brother and sister while her mother ran the streets. April took her frustration out on people at school that she was jealous of or who made fun of her.

She even continued to act out once they were rescued by their grandmother. The estranged relationship between her mother and grandmother meant that they didn't get to see her for a couple of years. So when Grandma showed up unannounced at their door telling them to pack a bag and come with her, April rebelled against the abrupt changes to her world. Suddenly someone was there to make sure she went to school and did her homework every day. And April and her siblings came home to a clean house, ate dinner at the table as a family, and had regular bedtimes. But the toughest change was going to church all the time. That is until she joined the choir. April loved to sing. She got to sing at church which meant she liked going to church now, especially when it was her turn to belt out a solo. And once she finally got used to her grandmother's rule and talked to her therapist about the importance of following them, she stopped being so rebellious.

Adjusted to the rules at home, April was now adjusting to the people at her new school. Some of them probably looked down on her for being a Black girl from the hood so they stayed away from her. Then there were others that randomly approached her and asked stupid questions like, "Can I touch your hair?" They acted like she was from a different planet instead of across town.

Robin snapped her fingers in front of April's face. "Earth to April."

April tilted her head and stared at Robin.

"I called your name three times. Don't worry about them. You can come hang out with me this weekend. Maybe we can go get some pizza and go to the movies or something."

April raised her eyebrow. "What makes you think I want to hang out with you either?"

Robin narrowed her eyes and glared at her. "You know I'm the only one around here who likes you. Maybe you should stop treating me like crap." She picked her tray up and was about to leave their table.

"Stop being so dramatic" April let out a big sigh. "Sit down," April relented. When her friend didn't comply she asked her again nicely. "Please." She finally eased back down. April grumbled, "Sorry. I'm just not used to hanging around White people."

Robin rolled her eyes. Something she learned from her. It caused a smirk to appear on April's face.

"Okay. I'll ask my grandma if I can come over to your house Saturday. They both smiled and finished their lunch.

14

Felicia hoped that her mother wouldn't give her any problems about seeing her kids. She had already been through a lot. Missing her kids was driving her crazy which is why she took this job so she could have money to take care of them. It wasn't easy being in your thirties with no job history. She practically begged the manager for this job. Felicia wasn't the typical twenty-something girl that worked there with a big behind, fake breasts, and a weave half way down her back. But she was still good looking and shapely despite once being a crackhead. He must've felt sorry for her or needed her for a little variety in the club. Either way, she had her first real job so she was ecstatic.

She knew that she was going to make good money, but she didn't realize that first she had to spend some money. In Atlanta, it costs to get an adult entertainment permit. Everyone in the club had to have one, even the owner. That didn't include the processing fee or the fingerprint charge. They also ran a background check. Since she didn't have any outstanding charges and hadn't been arrested for distributing drugs, she passed.

Once she finished training with another waitress for a couple shifts, she was finally given a section of the club to work on her own. It felt exciting to earn two hundred dollars on her first night. By the end of her second shift she had enough money to pay back her friend that loaned her the money she needed to get started in the first place. Everything she earned after that was going to be for bills and to get her kids back. But what didn't feel good was her feet. Working all night in stilettos was killing her. But they were part of the uniform because men loved to see women in heels. The only thing she could do was soak her sore feet in warm water and Epsom Salt after work every day like she remembered her mother doing when she was little and pray that she didn't get any painful blisters.

But her feet weren't the only issues on the job. Felicia hadn't figured out what was worse yet, dealing with the strippers and their bad attitudes or tolerating the male customers. She didn't make a good first impression with the dancers. It all started when the waitress that was training her took her in the back to meet everyone. First, she was introduced to the middle-aged house mom that was telling a couple dancers to go back out on the floor. Then to a pleasant fully dressed woman trying to sell skimpy costumes to the strippers. The dancers were busy doing each other's hair and makeup and didn't even bother to look up to see who they were being introduced to. Usually, Felicia only saw other naked women in the shower. So walking in a room full of naked women was a little uncomfortable to her, but she knew that she'd better hurry and get used to it.

Felicia noticed towels on the chairs but didn't think much of it, figuring that maybe the chairs were hard or old and raggedy. Since her feet were already hurting, she sat down while the waitress and one of the dancers gossiped. Before she could get comfortable, the towel was yanked from underneath her. Everything in the room went deathly silent and all the ladies were now staring at her like she had an extra nose in the center of her forehead. Felicia looked back and forth between the stripper who grabbed the towel and the waitress for one of them to explain what just happened. The dancer yelled, "You sat on my towel."

"Okay," she said slowly breaking the word down by syllable. She lifted up her hands and looked to her trainer for further explanation.

The house mom walked over to the upset stripper. Her trainer abruptly ended her conversation and ushered Felicia back out to the club. When Felicia asked what she did wrong she was informed, "You don't sit down on anybody's towel here. The dancers use their towels to wipe themselves down and put on the chairs so they aren't sitting on them naked after each other. And you just offended her by sitting on her towel."

"How was I supposed to know that? She could have said excuse me though instead of snatching it from under me. I ain't trying to go back to jail, but I've gotten into fights over less crap than that," Felicia confessed as she huffed and picked up a tray to get back to work.

Her trainer grabbed her shoulder. Felicia faced her and saw a look of curiosity in her eyes. "What did you go to jail for?"

Felicia closed her eyes realizing that her emotions had caused her to run her mouth. She hadn't planned on telling anyone at her job about being in jail or rehab. "Nothing. Never mind. Can we get back to work please?" she answered and made a quick exit in the other direction.

Then there were the men. Felicia was beginning to see the different types of men who hung out there. There were the dope boys with a never-ending supply of money to shower down on the girl. The younger clientele were officially grown, but acted like little boys who had never seen naked women before, especially if they were in a large group. The more of them there were, the more they pumped each other up. They weren't supposed to touch the dancers or waitresses, but they got away with as much as they could without getting kicked out of the club. The older ones were less rowdy and more laid back. They arrived solo or with a much smaller group of men. But the amount of money they threw at the dancers was ridiculous as well. A lot of them wore wedding rings which made her wonder if their wives knew where they were or how much money they were spending on females they didn't even know. Were their kids at home with holes in the bottom of their shoes wearing high water pants? Did their wife have to stretch the grocery budget and rob Peter to pay Paul with the household bills while her man was out making it rain because a performer could swing upside down on a chrome stripper pole and their wives couldn't? Felicia could only imagine what the men were whispering in their ears when they were giving them lap dances.

But her job was simply to make all of them happy by getting them their drinks and food as quickly as she could. She began to recognize the regulars and brought their favorite drinks to them before they even ordered it. Sometimes they even had brief conversations. They liked her so they tipped well which meant she liked them. Even though some of her customers asked her out, she told herself that she wouldn't date anyone that she met there because she didn't want any man of hers regularly hanging out in strip clubs and giving money to naked women.

But there was one dark skinned guy with a goatee and plenty of tattoos covering his huge muscles who sat in her section and flirted with her every time he came in. He sat by the TV near the bar and watched sports. She never saw Michael getting dances from the girls. He seemed a lot more interested in eating hot wings and watching sports than having naked women gyrating their behind in his face. That fact alone made him stand out from the rest of the jokers who hung out there. Some other things she noticed was that he never drank more than the two-drink minimum no matter how long he was there, he always had a big wad of cash and tipped her well. He was definitely her type. She couldn't resist a fine chocolate man. And she was lonely. It had been a long time since she went to bed and woke up with a man lying next to her. Plus, he knew where she worked and didn't care. Overhearing horror stories about guys dumping the other employees as soon as they found out where they worked, made her think that having a relationship while she was employed at Stiletto was out of the question. Felicia wasn't sure if she would turn him down if he asked her out again. *Maybe I can have some fun with him for a little while until I get my kids back. He'll probably run scared when he finds out that I have three kids anyway.*

Part Two

Like You Need a Hole in Your Head

15

As Mary pulled up the driveway with a trunk full of groceries for Thanksgiving dinner later this week, her cell phone rang. "Hey baby. What's going on?"

"My friend Walter has two tickets to the Falcons game tonight. He asked me if I wanted to go. We didn't have any plans, did we?"

Mary sighed. "Who is this Walter guy that keeps coming up?"

"I told you. He is a friend of mine." Mary could hear that he was getting annoyed with her for asking one simple question. She didn't care because she was upset with him as well.

"Well how come I've never met him?"

"I haven't known him that long. You'll meet him soon." They were both quiet for a moment. "Look, I haven't been to a football game in a while, so I'll see you when I get home later."

"You know, you have been going out a lot lately. Is there something I need to know?"

"No. You know everything you need to know, baby," he answered.

She got out of her Jag and slammed the door behind her. Ready to end this call, she grabbed a bag and remarked, "I didn't sign up for this."

"You didn't sign up for what Mary?" Not giving her a chance to answer he proclaimed, "And I didn't sign up to be questioned about my every move." Now they were both yelling.

"Well when your moves include coming home at one or two o'clock in the morning you'd better believe that your wife is going to have questions."

She could hear him breathing heavily into the phone. "I just called to tell you I'm going out. I didn't call to argue. But I see everything has to be an argument with you these days."

Mary was standing outside her car. The midday temperature was only fifty-two degrees, but she could feel sweat beginning to run down her back. But she was too aggravated to sit back down in her car. At the same time, she knew she couldn't juggle the heavy bags of food and her phone. Mary desperately wanted to get her point across and convince her husband that they should still be celebrating being newlyweds instead of having issues that young people who have never been married before might have. "Don't try and make this all my fault that you are suddenly spending more time away from home. When we were dating, you didn't act like this."

"Baby, you are making a big deal out of nothing. I'm going to a football game with a friend and then I'm coming straight home to you."

Mary gave up when she felt tears come to her eyes. "Okay. I'll see you when you get home." She hung up the phone before he could respond.

She wasn't sure what was going on with her husband. Lately, he had been going places on the days that she didn't help out at the church. He even insisted that they take separate cars on the days that she was scheduled to work at Mt. Zion. He said it was just in case there was an emergency with one of the church members and he needed to go see about them in a hurry. Zachariah also suggested that there could be an emergency with the kids at the school that she might have to leave him to take care of. He claimed that driving two cars would alleviate any problems. But Mary didn't believe him. So far there hadn't been any situations like the ones he offered as examples. However, she did notice him nudging her to go home earlier than him and get started on dinner.

He was always telling her that he loved having her at the church with him when they were dating and lived in separate houses. Had living and working together made him sick of her already? She had heard horror stories about couples who were in similar situations. They spent all of their time together. It worked for a while, but turned into a nightmare at the end. Mary was determined that she was not going to let that happen to them. So she agreed to drive her own car when she went to the church every other day even though she would much rather enjoy his company in the car. There was always someone at the church with them and at least one of the kids was always at home. Riding to Mt. Zion during the week had been their only alone time. And he wanted to take it away from them. She desperately wanted to know why.

Once she made a third trip to get the rest of the plastic grocery bags, she dropped them on the kitchen counter harder than she intended to. Mary hoped the carton of eggs wasn't in one of those bags. The refrigerator and freezer doors were wide open so she finally felt a little relief on her skin as she moved around the room that usually gave her so much joy. On the inside, she was so angry that she could hardly see straight. Ever since his friends died, Zachariah had been going out three or four times a week with a new friend that she didn't even know and coming home later than any married man or minister should. And when he did come in, she could smell the alcohol on him when he tried to get intimate with her, even though he tried to mask the smell with a mint.

Everyone knows that Jesus changed water into wine

and drank on occasion in the Bible. But Christians are not supposed to drink in excess. Zachariah was getting drunk. When she questioned him, he would slur and give incoherent answers. And they couldn't finish a conversation because five minutes after he tiptoed into their bedroom, he was passed out, snoring, and drooling. She wondered why he bothered to creep in when he probably woke the entire house up when he used the garage door opener to park his Mercedes in the garage. But Mary reasoned that he was too intoxicated to make sound decisions including driving himself home under the influence.

Had she made the biggest mistake of her life marrying him? They did have a quick courtship. But seeing him at church all these years, Mary thought Zachariah was different. How could he act one way at Mt. Zion and then turn around and act completely different somewhere else?

She obviously had an "I attract drunk husbands" tattoo stamped across her forehead. Life with her first husband consisted of lies, alcohol, and other women. He stopped at the bar to have a drink on his way home from work every single day once she was big and pregnant with Felicia. She remembered complaining to a friend and hearing, "That's when the dirty bastards know that you aren't going to leave them and start doing things that they weren't doing before. They all do it. No sense in getting yourself all worked up about it. Men will be men." Mary always hated that saying. It was just an excuse for childish men to get away with bad behavior. She was much younger when she dealt with her first husband's foolishness. Fear of being a single mom caused her to stay and put up with his mess until old age and too much drinking began to take their toll on his health and he finally settled down and started acting like a halfway decent husband. She couldn't wait years for Zachariah to settle down once he got older and his health started failing him. His doctor already had him on Lisinopril for high blood pressure and Simvastatin to lower his cholesterol. So he knew he shouldn't be drinking while he was taking medicine anyway.

Mary was much older and had three grandkids to worry about now. She tried her best not to argue with him in front of them. She wasn't sure if the kids were aware of what was going on yet. But they were smart kids. So if they knew, she didn't want Anthony Jr. to think that it was okay for men to treat women like this. And she definitely didn't want the girls to think that women had to tolerate being treated poorly either.

Has the stress of raising someone else's kids when you are sixty been too much for Zachariah? Or did they get married too soon after his wife passed away? Was he one of those men who loved the chase and now that he had her, had he lost interest? Mary didn't know what her husband was up to, but she planned to find out. They had barely gotten past the scandal with Joshua and April. Imagine if someone in the congregation saw him drunk. It would ruin his reputation.

"Father, I realize that you know what you are doing even when it's not clear to us, but I don't know what you want me to do. So God please keep my family together.

Teach us to be more like you want us to be. Please help my husband and daughter find their way, Lord." Mary stopped talking and wiped the tears off her face with the back of her hand.

Suddenly, the bags shifted and pomegranates started rolling off the marble countertop and onto the floor. Mary realized that she had been standing in the same spot and needed to put away the groceries before the kid's vanilla ice cream she bought to go with her pies started melting all over the place. As she retrieved the frozen items from the bags, she was determined to figure out how to make Zachariah stop his destructive behavior so it wouldn't destroy their family or bring down the church.

16

It had been a long day. Zachariah just finished working with the new audio-visual volunteers to sync his sermon with their PowerPoint presentation. This was another change implemented by Donald. Zachariah only agreed to it because they already had a projection screen that came down from the ceiling behind the choir stand that they rarely used. Donald convinced him that they had members who were experienced in graphic design and multimedia that were willing to volunteer their time on Sundays so it wouldn't cost the church anything. But Zachariah insisted that he get to watch a video of his sermon. If he decided that the presentation didn't meet his standards or was in any way a distraction from the word, Sunday would be the first and last time they would do this.

Earlier today, he and the assistant pastor also had a long meeting to discuss other changes at Zion. At some points it became a heated debate. Zachariah raised his voice to bring his point home to Donald, "This is the way we've always done it and I don't see any reason to change."

"With all due respect Pastor, when I interviewed for this job, I told you that I was going to recommend changes that I thought would move this church forward and grow membership. You said that you would be open to a few changes. Well hasn't my suggestion to open up another church service brought in over two hundred new members?"

Zachariah had to hand it to Donald. His advice about an earlier service had paid off. But what he was suggesting now wasn't going to work. "Yes, you have been able to bring in new members just like you promised you would. And I agreed to the media ministry that you advised. But I've already tried hiring a full-time secretary before and it didn't work."

"That's because you were too busy to weed through a bunch of candidates so you hired a temp agency. But I would be in charge of finding someone qualified. So how about I conduct the first round of interviews and get you three experienced applicants for you to have a second interview with. That way the final selection would be totally up to you."

Zachariah rubbed his chin. "I don't know."

Donald continued, "I don't understand your

resistance. There's no reason for a church this size not to have a full-time secretary to support it. Sure your wife is doing a great job, but now that she is first lady she has other duties that she could be doing. Isn't it traditional for the first lady to be in charge of the annual Women's Day Event? She could also relieve you of some of the sick and shut-in visits that you do. And aren't you the one who told me stories of how the former first lady would drive some of our elderly members to the grocery store who insisted upon taking care of themselves when everyone could see that they needed help? She would patiently go up and down all the aisles with them until they had everything that they wanted. If the first lady doesn't want to do that, there are plenty of other things that she could do."

They were both silent for a minute. Zachariah noticed that Donald's lips began to curl up. He seemed pleased that he was quiet and at least considering his idea. But then Zachariah began to shake his head. "How am I going to tell my wife that she is being replaced by a stranger?"

"But you said yourself that she needed to step up and take over the women's ministry. Can't you tell her that you are freeing her up to do that and some other first lady duties?"

Zachariah threw his hand up to stop Donald from continuing. "Okay. You're right."

"Great. I'll post the job in a couple of newspapers and start interviewing as soon as I receive some resumes that I like."

Starting to laugh, Zachariah noticed that Donald stopped smiling and was staring at him like he was losing it so he explained. "I just realized that I'm going to be sleeping on the couch tonight because of your bright idea."

Not in a hurry to go home and inform his wife that her services in the church office were no longer needed, Zachariah stopped at his favorite bar again. He had started convincing himself that no matter what Mary thought, it was no big deal to come to the bar two or three times a week. It was okay for him to socialize with people that weren't necessarily church folks sometimes. After all, Jesus spent more of his time on Earth with sinners than he did with religious folks.

Walter was glued to his usual spot drinking a beer and watching reruns of old football games from the late eighties on the sports channel. They gave each other a pound on their fists as Zachariah joined him. "Bacardi Rum and Coke with no ice, right?" He looked up and noticed one of the cute regular bartenders putting down a drink napkin and smiling at him.

"Yeah. Thanks."

She nodded her head and started pouring his drink. He took a big gulp of it as soon as she slid it in front of him and exhaled. A few minutes later his phone started buzzing. He sighed when Mary's name came across the screen, but he didn't pick up. He felt Walter looking over at him from the corner of his eye. "Man ain't you gonna answer that?"

Zachariah shook his head. "She's getting so that she

expects me home by a certain time and if I'm not there then she starts calling me every thirty minutes. Well I never told her that I get off at a certain time. I stop working when my work is done."

"Whatever you say man," Walter said, shaking his head. "I'm single. Don't let hanging out with me get you in trouble with your brand-new wife."

"I'll call her back in a minute," he lied to himself.

Mary kept calling every fifteen minutes so he finally answered. She immediately started bombarding him with questions. "When are you coming home? I've been calling the church phone and your cell phone. Why aren't you answering my calls? The kids ate already, but I've been waiting to eat dinner with you. Are you out drinking again?"

He didn't want to lie so he avoided a couple of the questions and simply replied that he would be home soon then flipped his phone closed before she had an opportunity to respond. But he did hear it ring several more times. Sensing that he was already in the doghouse, he reasoned that there was no cause to rush home now. If his wife wanted to quarrel with him, it was going to be after this bar closed because he didn't intend to hop off this stool anytime soon.

"Another rum and Coke please. And I'll take an order of ribs with fries too."

17

"Why aren't you getting up? Are you sick or something?"

Mary rolled over in bed ignoring his questions.

He adjusted his tie and raised his voice a little. "Did you hear me?"

She turned back over, staring him directly in his eyes. "Yes, I heard you. No, I'm not sick. I just don't feel like playing this charade today. So I'm not going to church."

Zachariah stepped back and squinted his eyes. "What are you talking about? What charade, Mary?"

"This one big happy family sham. The one where we are deeply in love with no problems," she answered with a sarcastic tone.

"Baby, the first year of marriage is always the hardest. No one expects us not to have any struggles."

Mary fired back, "No one expects their pastor to have a drinking problem either."

Zachariah threw up his hand like a cop directing traffic for her to be quiet. "Stop saying that stupid crap about me. I don't have a drinking problem. I can go days without even thinking about drinking. You don't know what you are talking about." Closing his eyes, he massaged the bridge of his nose. Suddenly his head began pounding. "It's too early in the morning for this foolishness Mary. So get out the bed and wake the kids up so y'all won't be late for the second service."

She fluffed the pillow against the headboard and sat up. "Don't act like I'm causing you to have a headache. We both know that it's a hangover. You'd better get a few teaspoons of honey before you go inside the house of the Lord." Mary folded her arms in front of her. "I'm not going to church and act like things are fine when you just got home a few hours ago."

"You haven't missed a service at Mt. Zion in years, Mary. So you wait until I make you the first lady to decide not to come?"

Mary's head snapped back. "Until you made me first lady? I don't like the way that sounded." She blinked her eyes and shook her head. Now yelling she said, "No, I didn't wait until you made me first lady to decide to miss church. I waited until it caused my skin to crawl and almost threw up in my own mouth to have to stare up at you in the pulpit and act like I still respect you to skip church."

Zachariah was too stunned to move. Did his bride just tell him that she didn't respect him anymore? After a few seconds of staring each other down, he forced himself to put one foot in front of the other and exit the room before he did or said something that he wouldn't be able to take back. He was so angry that the entire house shook when he slammed the door to the garage on his way out.

Driving to church knowing that Mary was serious and wasn't going to change her mind about showing up, Zachariah decided to bend the truth if anyone asked where she was. He would say that two of the kids were sick so Mary had to stay home with them. After all, Brooklyn was sneezing this weekend. So it was probably only a matter of time before everyone in the house was sick too.

Once he calmed down and came up with his plan, it wasn't long before he started yawning. Zachariah stayed out later than he intended to last night. Mary was usually in bed when he came home late. But last night she was waiting up to confront him in the kitchen. They argued for a while until he had enough and stormed into the master bathroom to get away from her. This turned out to be a good thing because he got sick as soon as he crossed the threshold. Being persistent, Mary followed him in the bathroom right on his heels. She quickly did a U-turn when she spotted him leaning head first over the commode. He threw up so much that he didn't have anything left in him and it physically hurt when he heaved.

Zachariah woke up in the fetal position next to the toilet with a blanket over him. He was still fully dressed with his shoes on. Checking his watch, he realized that several hours had passed, but he didn't even remember lying down on the bathroom floor. Apparently his wife cared enough to cover him up, but not enough to wake him up to get in their bed. He struggled to pull himself up by the marble countertop. When he lifted his head and saw his bloodshot eyes and a dry trail of drool down the side of his face. He searched the medicine cabinet for eye drops and moved as quickly as he could to get in the shower and clean up.

At a red light, he put the Benz in park and unhooked his seatbelt to be able to reach the flask in his glove compartment. One swig should be all he needed to wake him up and shake the memory from this morning. It wasn't until he put his seatbelt back on and pulled away from the light that he looked around to make sure that no one saw him through his tinted windows. Zachariah popped a peppermint in his mouth to mask the smell of the rum from anyone that got in his personal space.

By the time he pulled into his parking spot on the side of the church, he started wondering if Mary was going to take a stand and continue to miss church service every week. Deciding that his new wife wasn't going to make him look bad in front of the entire congregation, he resolved to go home after church and make up with her even though she was the one messing up a good thing, not him. She was the one who didn't have any empathy for a man who had lost a wife and two close friends back to back. Sure he went out and had a couple drinks, but that's all he did. He paid all the bills, didn't put his hands on her or the kids, wasn't cheating on her, and always came home to her every night. What more did she want? Maybe if he stayed home more this week, that would get her off his back and she'd be happy that he was trying.

A couple good nights of sleep couldn't hurt either. Zachariah had to admit that he wasn't a young man anymore. He couldn't hang like he used to before he decided to dedicate his life to the Lord. Socializing made him forget about all his problems temporarily, but he was exhausted trying to survive off only a few hours of sleep several times a week. Donald even caught him taking a nap at his desk twice last week. He tried to act like he and Mary had stayed up acting like newlyweds which was so far from the truth he was surprised God didn't strike him down for lying in His house. Seemed like she was always mad at him and not in the mood to make love anymore. When he did convince her to have sex with him, she just laid there like a dry piece of toast with no jelly.

Later that afternoon, Zachariah sat in his office busying himself with paperwork. He wasn't in any big hurry to go home. So he was going to wait until the traffic jam getting out of the parking lot after the second service was cleared up before he headed out. He knew the parking lot crew would clear a path for him though. When there was an unexpected knock at the door, he assumed it was the assistant pastor or one of the deacons and didn't bother getting up. "Come in."

The second he saw her short curly hair when she stuck her head in the door, Zachariah grimaced. He knew he made a big mistake not asking who it was. "Hi Pastor. That was a great sermon today," she cheerfully said, letting herself in and quickly shutting the office door behind her. In walked the woman in the senior choir who was always flirting with him. She pestered him so much that he should know her name by heart, but it always escaped him. Being a faithful member of the choir for several years, it made him uncomfortable thinking about asking her what her name was. If she wasn't so pesky he would look forward to their encounters and gladly remember her name, like he did everyone else's.

"Thanks. What can I help you with today?" He hoped that his all business tone would ward off any attempt to try to seduce him.

"Oh I just noticed that you were here alone today." She batted her eyelashes and ran her hand down her thigh. Zachariah couldn't help but notice how short and tight her skirt was underneath her open choir robe. "Is everything okay at home?"

Zachariah promptly stood up and began gathering his belongings hoping she would get the hint. "Yes, nothing major. A couple sick grandkids, that's all."

"That's right. You've got a house full of little germy kids now. You need to keep your distance from them. I sure would hate for you to catch anything."

Stifling a laugh at her concern for him, Zachariah replied, "Thanks. I'll be fine."

He could hear the friction from her stockings rubbing together on her thighs as she eased closer to him. "Well there's never been any doubt about how fine you are," she gushed and winked at him.

Zachariah stepped away from her and cleared his throat. He looked over her head at the door to keep his eyes off her body. Despite the fact that her aggressive behavior was a turn-off for him, she was an attractive woman. Not to mention that his wife hadn't been performing her wifely duties lately. "I don't mean to be rude, but I was actually on my way home when you knocked."

His admirer was close enough so that Zachariah could hear her sigh before she responded. She looked over his desk, grabbed a pen and wrote down ten digits on a blank sheet of paper. "Okay then Pastor. I won't hold you up. But if you need a place to get away from all the germs at your house, you let me know." With that she slowly turned on her heels and left his office as he tried not to notice the middle part of her choir robe swaying.

Zachariah shook his head and smiled. He had to give it to her, she was persistent. She had been trying to seduce him since his first wife was ill. And the fact that he had ignored her and married Mary didn't appear to break her spirit. In fact, she had gotten bolder. He decided to give it a few more minutes before he headed out for home to make sure that the coast was clear.

If Mary knew that a couple of their female members were still trying to hit on him even though they were married, she wouldn't skip any more services. She was lucky that he was a faithful man. Plenty of other men, even a few of his minister friends, would take advantage of the opportunities being thrown at them. She was at home pouting about him having a few drinks a couple times a week when he could be doing so many other things that would be detrimental to their marriage vows. He worked hard and wasn't hurting anyone by making a stop to wind down from a stressful workday. But Zachariah was headed home to try and keep the peace.

18

"Wow. My kids live here now?" Felicia drove up the circular driveway of her mother's house in slow motion. She was in awe of the well-manicured bushes that lined the perimeter of the vast property. When her mother gave her their address and said it was off Cascade Road, Felicia had no idea the house would be a mini mansion. "Pastor Williams must be making a lot more money than I thought he was." She parked her raggedy 1985 Chevy Nova behind what looked like a shiny brand new 1991 Jaguar. Felicia assumed that it was her mother's car because she knew Pastor always drove a Mercedes. The grass was still a lively bright green even though the leaves were falling off the surrounding trees. It was well manicured like they had a crew of landscapers that came on a regular basis. She took it all in with envy as she tried to smooth the wrinkles out her pants as she walked up the stone walkway to the porch.

Felicia was admiring the Christmas wreath, so before she had a chance to ring the doorbell, Brooklyn swung the massive door open and practically knocked her down jumping up into her arms. Tears rolled down Felicia's face hearing her baby say how much she missed her. Anthony Jr. was the next child to appear. Felicia walked into the house barely able to hold her growing child who was still up in her arms. When Brooklyn slid down, Anthony gave her a big hug too. "You look good Mama."

"Thank you, baby. So do you."

"Thanks. I'm finally taller than you now," he announced with a big smile on his face.

Felicia laughed. "You wish. Brooklyn, is your brother taller than me?"

Brooklyn stepped back and waited for them to get in the familiar position. She examined her mother and brother standing back-to-back. Her youngest child smiled and answered, "Yep. He's finally taller than you, Mama."

Felicia gave a fake pout but then a big grin spread across his face. Jr. had been claiming to be taller than her for years. And now her only son was in fact taller than her. She kissed him on the forehead. She jokingly asked, "How much did you pay your little sister to lie for you? I think y'all had this planned out before I got here."

Brooklyn laughed and shook her head. Anthony

said, "Don't be mad. You are still taller than Brooklyn."

Eventually, April walked down the stairs and joined them in the foyer. "Hey baby."

"Hi," she replied without looking directly at her mother.

The energy in the room instantly shifted and everything was still. And their grandmother entering didn't help any. "So, you made it."

Felicia nodded her head.

"Did you have any trouble finding the house?"

"No. Your directions led me right to your door." She looked around as far as she could see and commented, "Your house is beautiful, Mom."

"Oh thanks. I've still got a few things left to do, but we've settled in pretty good." The room was quiet for a few awkward seconds.

"Grandma, can I show Mommy my room?"

Her mother looked back and forth between Brooklyn and her. Felicia thought *surely she can't be scared to let me walk around her house like I might steal something. Can't she tell by the way that I look that I am finally off drugs?* Felicia was surprised that her mother didn't jump at the chance to show her how great her kids had it without her.

Mary slowly smiled at her innocent grandbaby and

simply said, "Of course you can."

April moved out of the way before her anxious little sister ran her over. Felicia was being pulled closely behind her, because Brooklyn had a firm grip on her hand. That didn't stop Felicia from slowing to kiss April on the cheek. Unfortunately, she saw her first born coldly wipe the kiss off with the back of her hand out of the corner of her eye. Felicia noticed that April didn't greet her with the same excitement as her other two kids. She knew that it was going to take some time to rebuild the tight mother-daughter relationship that they once had before Anthony Sr. walked out and their lives fell apart. But she was back and she wasn't going away ever again.

It appeared that the kids had the entire upstairs to themselves. Each of them had their own bedroom. Practically everything in Brooklyn's room was pink, her favorite color. There were so many stuffed animals on her bed that Felicia knew it took her five minutes just to line them up neatly in the morning. But her bed was the only thing with excess. Nothing else in the room was messy or out of place. She only had a few books and family pictures on her dresser. Felicia remembered never having to yell at her baby to make her bed or clean her room. Brooklyn seemed to come out of her womb a neat freak.

April's room was completely different. Her dirty clothes and a couple pairs of shoes were scattered across her carpet. The closet door was open revealing clothes thrown on the shelf, falling off the hangers, and shoes and boots tossed on the floor. Felicia also noticed a school uniform lying on the chair in the corner. She took a mental note to ask the kids where they went to school now while they ate lunch. The walls were painted a dark purple but they were almost totally covered with posters and pictures of celebrities ripped out of magazines.

But Anthony's room was the worst. Neither one of them entered his room. From the doorway Felicia could see three glasses half full with different colors of liquid in them on his nightstand. His pajamas and the covers from his bed were all tangled up on the floor. And video games and controllers were scattered on the floor in front of his TV. Felicia shook her head. Her baby boy was still a slob. She lowered her voice and asked, "Does your grandmother come up here?"

Brooklyn whispered, "She only comes up to wake us up for school."

"And she doesn't fuss about his room being like that?"

Brooklyn pulled her mother along talking over her shoulder. "She used to. But he knows the maid is going to come clean it up so he doesn't bother."

Maid? They have a maid now too?

No longer whispering, Brooklyn exclaimed, "Come on. I'll show you the rest of the house. Wait until you see the basement."

Brooklyn was right. The modern kitchen, and her mother's master bedroom were really nice. The Christmas tree that had to be at least ten feet tall that was surrounded by neatly wrapped presents in the living room was not missed by her. But her mouth dropped when she walked down to the bottom level. It was big enough to be a separate house. The kids had their very own movie theater and game room right in the basement. How was she going to be able to convince them to move back into a tiny apartment with her after living here? But she couldn't think about that now. First things first. She planned on taking them to lunch and to Greenbriar Mall so they could spend some quality time together. She was prepared to answer any questions they may have for her or just hang out as a family. Brooklyn and Anthony would probably keep quiet and enjoy the day. Suspecting that April wouldn't let her off that easily, Felicia had already braced herself for her teenage daughter's rage.

When they walked back up the basement stairs, Mary was waiting for them. "It's eleven fifteen now. When do you plan on bringing them back home?"

Felicia didn't like the way her mother emphasized the word home. Her kids were not home. But she tried to speak with respect in her usual tone anyway when she answered. "In a few hours. I just wanted to get something to eat and take them to the mall."

"We just ate," April interjected towards the small group from the foyer.

"Then we will go to the mall first." Felicia answered without hesitation to squash her child's attempt not to spend time with her. She was looking at her mother, but she could feel April's eyes burning into her skin. So she turned to glare at her. If she wanted to have this conversation standing up in the living room right here right now, Felicia was ready.

Her mother must have noticed the tension so she spoke up. "Okay. I'll be right here waiting on them. But if for some reason I have to step out for a minute, they all have keys."

Brooklyn kissed her grandmother and turned to grab her hand again. "Bye Grandma," she yelled over her shoulder as she led her mother toward the front door. Anthony immediately followed behind them. But Felicia could hear her mother instructing April to go and behave herself. She hoped that her eldest daughter would obey her grandmother, otherwise today was going to be a long day.

19

By the time April walked outside, her brother and sister were sitting eagerly in the backseat. She had trained them well. As the oldest she deserved to ride shotgun. But she had no desire to sit next to her mother so she opened her sister's door. "Sit up front." Confused, Brooklyn stared at her for a second, but quickly smiled and did as she was told.

Still sitting in the driveway, her mother was looking at her with questioning eyes through her rear-view mirror. April glared back at her daring her to say anything out loud. She wanted to make it crystal clear to everyone that she did not want to be on this sham of a family outing. And if her mother did confront her she was going to tell her off, jump out of the car, and explain to her grandmother that she just couldn't deal with her today. But her mother slowly pulled out the driveway without saying a word to her.

Brooklyn was enjoying her seat next to their mother. She was raving about all her new teachers and friends at Grove Wood Academy. April rolled her eyes. Unlike her, her perky little sister was enjoying her experience there. When their mother asked Anthony about his classes, he talked briefly about them and said that they were okay. "What about you April? How are you doing at school?"

"Report cards haven't come out yet."

"Okay, but how do you think you are doing so far?" Her mother pushed.

They were stopped at a light. Even without looking in her direction, April knew that her mother was watching her again through the mirror. So she shrugged her shoulders. She could hear Felicia sigh, but she obviously wasn't going to give up trying. "Do you like the teachers? Have you met any new friends?"

April decided to answer her questions so she would leave her alone. "The teachers are okay I guess. Everyone there is White."

"Who says you can't have White friends?"

April shook her head and continued to look at the passing scenery through the backseat window. She had answered this woman's questions, yet she was still bothering her.

"I know we didn't have many White people in our neighborhood. But when you get a job, you are going to have to work around them. So you might as well get used to it. They are people just like us. Don't let them intimidate you."

"Who said I'm intimidated?" April snapped and searched for her mother's eyes in the mirror but couldn't find them. "I can sing and act better than all the other girls in my drama class. And this is my first time, but they've been doing this for years. I'm even going to audition for the lead in our spring musical."

"That's great. You are just as smart as they are too, no matter what anyone says."

Her nosey sister stuck her head between the seat and the window to face her, "What about that girl I see you with after school April? Isn't she your friend?"

"You mean Robin?" She tilted her head to the side and stared at the ceiling of the car. April hadn't really thought about it before, but if she did have one friend at her school it was Robin. She shrugged her shoulders and admitted, "I guess so." That was enough of an answer for her sister to turn back around.

"Oh so you are making friends over there. That's good." Except for the radio and the wind from the cracked windows, the car was quiet again momentarily. "I found a job so that I can take care of us. So we are going to have to figure out how you three can keep going to your new school when you move back in with me."

"When we what?" April must have heard her mother wrong. She couldn't possibly think that they would want to come live with her again after what she had put them through. First, she was never home to take care of them. Leaving April in charge to cook dinner and get them off to school for days at a time while she was out getting high. Then she went to jail. When she got out, she extorted money from Pastor and Joshua to start getting high again. And on top of all that, she disappeared for almost a year. Now she had the audacity to show up with no explanation and tell them that they were moving back with her.

"When you move back in with me," she said matter-of-factly. Their mom paused for a second before continuing. "I'm working and saving money for us right now so it won't be long."

April turned to her brother to see if he was hearing what she was saying. But he was playing his handheld video game already. Brooklyn curiously asked, "Where are we going to live? Are you going to get our old apartment back?"

This can't be happening. Had her grandmother agreed to this behind her back?

"No, I'm going to find someplace else for us to live. We need a fresh start."

April hit her brother's arm for him to snap out of it and pay attention. Then she yelled, "We're doing just fine

where we are. We don't want to come live with you."
There were those eyes staring at her through the rear view
mirror again. April waited for her little sister or brother to
chime in, but of course they didn't. They came to rely on
her to handle tricky situations the last couple of years. It
suddenly felt suffocating in the small car. A claustrophobic
person would be losing their mind at that moment.

Her mom blinked and then turned away. "We'll talk
about this some other time. Today, I just want to catch up
with my babies and grab something to eat." She reached
over and touched Brooklyn's leg causing her to turn to her
and smile.

*Could her mother really force them to come back
and live with her?* It took some time, but April had come to
forgive her grandmother for making her feel abandoned by
her too. She didn't know that conditions were as bad as
they were at their apartment because April didn't let
anyone know. But they had moved past that and had a
normal grandmother-granddaughter relationship now. She
took good care of them. And as much as April hated to
admit it, they were a little spoiled. They had their own
bedrooms in a huge house, she drove her grandmother's old
car to school, she got almost everything she asked for, and
she had a few dollars in her pocket. She wondered where
her mother worked since she claimed to be able to take care
of them. April didn't remember her ever having a job
before. Not wanting to make her think that she was
interested in living with her, she repressed her desire to ask
her. Any other time, her nosey sister would have asked a
million questions. Where was she when April needed her?

"Mommy, where do you work?" April sucked her lips in to keep from smiling. She wanted to shout hallelujah. Her curious little sister finally came through for her.

"I found a job waiting tables. The tips are pretty good. It's hard on my feet though. But my babies are worth it." They were stopped at a light so their mom turned to look at them over her shoulder. Anthony still hadn't looked up from his game. So April composed herself and took this as an opportunity to look back at her like she was crazy. *Did her mother seriously think she could leave them, then show up and convince her that they were important to her again all of a sudden?*

20

"Are you firing me?" Mary yelled at Zachariah.

"Mary calm down and listen to what I'm telling you." His wife was lying in bed reading a book before they turned in for the night. The kids were already asleep, so he figured this was a good time to tell her. He had been procrastinating telling her all week that they had hired a full-time secretary who started the following day. If he didn't tell her now, she would show up for work and get the shock of her life when she saw Stacy sitting at her desk. "I've put off hiring a real secretary long enough. You helped me out and did a great job. But I have been picking up the slack all this time."

"A real secretary? Well what am I, chopped liver?" She was yelling so loud that she might wake the kids.

He was tired of reasoning with her. It was time to tell her the facts. "You started out as a part-time volunteer before I started paying you when you got the kids. But a church the size of Mt. Zion needs someone there full-time. Besides, you are the first lady now."

"What does that mean? I can't help out anymore because we're married." Zachariah tried to answer her but she kept shouting. "I've been volunteering at that church since it opened its door and now you are telling me that I have to stop?"

"That's not what I'm saying at all. If you would just shut your mouth and listen, you will find out what I'm saying." He yelled louder than he intended to. She slammed her book closed, folded her arms across her chest, and glared at him like she wished him harm. But at least she was finally quiet. "I'm saying that as first lady you have other duties."

"Like what?"

Zachariah held his hand up for her to stop talking again. "Like chairing the Women's Ministry. The annual Woman's Day Event is coming up soon and you need to be handling that."

For the first time since they started this conversation, Mary wasn't yelling. Her facial expression had changed from anger to fear. "But I've never led a ministry before or coordinated a big event like that. I don't know what to do. What if I mess it up this year?"

Zachariah was happy she wasn't hollering anymore.

He moved closer to her on the bed and held her hand. "You've done a fantastic job in every ministry that you've ever worked with. We didn't even have a Women's Day last year since -," Zachariah stopped talking mid-sentence. It never failed, every time he thought about death lately he got choked up. What he wanted to say was that since Mt. Zion didn't even have an event last year because his deceased wife wasn't there to kick it off, that the women would be so happy even if she didn't do a fantastic job, it was better than not having the annual event two years in a row.

Mary bit her bottom lip and said, "Okay. Don't worry. I've gone to every Women's Day Event over the years." She squeezed his hand and continued, "I can handle it. I'll do it." Zachariah breathed a sigh of relief. "But first I'll start helping you look for my replacement tomorrow."

And just like that, their short moment of peace was about to end. He closed his eyes for a second before confessing, "That won't be necessary. Donald and I already hired someone. Her name is Stacy and she starts tomorrow."

Mary forcefully snatched her hands away from his accidently scratching his palm. At least he assumed that it wasn't on purpose. "Wow. You don't have time to come home to eat dinner with your family or be here to support me when Felicia comes to pick up the kids, but you have time to hang out in the street until the middle of the night and hire a new secretary right under my nose."

Zachariah cupped his face in his hands and slowly

dragged his hands from his forehead to his chin. Of course things weren't as simple as she made them seem. Somehow the subject had changed from what she needed to do to what he wasn't doing. "Don't start this mess again Mary," he grumbled. "When I'm not here with you I'm working."

"Really?" Mary curled her lips. "You mean like the other night when I called you at midnight and you didn't answer?"

As far as he was concerned, he was the head of the household and was always going to have the final say on any disagreement. So no good could come from backing him in a corner. But he was going to remain quiet and let his wife say what she needed to say if it made her feel better.

She got up and started pacing the floor. "As a matter of fact, you are getting really good at never answering when I call you these days. If you were at Mt. Zion then why couldn't you pick up the phone?" She paused for a moment to allow him to answer, but he remained silent. At this point anything he said would be used against him. "Because you and I both know that you were not at the church or helping one of Mt. Zion's members. You've just been using working late as an excuse. You certainly haven't worked this late the entire time that I have known you."

Zachariah mumbled, "I didn't have a wife spending money faster than I could earn it the entire time you've known me either."

"What? Don't you dare try to turn this around on me," Mary shouted.

Leaning forward rubbing his hands on his knees, he decided that he wasn't going to take too much more of her hollering at him like he was a child in his own house. And for all her concern about the kids' welfare, shouldn't she be quiet so they could get some sleep?

Examining his wife glaring at him with her arms folded across her chest tapping one foot on the carpet, he knew she was ready for battle. Things had ended up turning ugly like he suspected they would and he wasn't going to spend the rest of the night arguing. So he slowly got up, maneuvered past Mary, and grabbed his cell phone and keys from his nightstand.

"Where do you think you're going?" Mary was actually bold enough to try and stop him. He had to yank his arm free from her tight grip. Without looking back, he kept walking toward the garage. "I know you weren't at work. You were out drinking. Isn't that why you never answer when I call you? Is that where you're going now? You need another drink like you need a hole in your head."

He could still hear Mary yelling in the house as he was backing out of the garage. By the time he got ready to push the button to close the garage door, she was coming out the house door into the garage moving towards him. As he pushed the button anyway, he hoped she had sense enough to stop and didn't follow him down the driveway. If she didn't, she would surely be locked out of the house in her robe and house shoes and have to ring the front doorbell to be let in by one of the kids. That's if they woke up. Hopefully, none of their neighbors were looking out the window to see her carrying on so foolishly in her pajamas. This wasn't the sweet woman that he married. His first wife had so much class that she would never try to embarrass him like this. Zachariah kept gazing in his rearview mirror to make sure that he wasn't being followed.

He called Walter to ask if it was okay if he dropped by. Unlike Zachariah's man cave in the basement which had been taken over by Mary's grandkids, his friend had a fully loaded bar. It was stocked with almost as much alcohol as the neighborhood restaurant, yet it was all going to waste because Walter didn't like drinking alone, and didn't like a bunch of people hanging out at his house anymore. Sometimes he would reminisce telling Zachariah about the epic house parties he and his wife used to have. He said he didn't have them anymore since she divorced him because they reminded him of the good times with her too much. But Walter invited him over one night when neither of them wanted to stop drinking when the restaurant closed. Tonight, Zachariah was going to help his buddy shake the dust off of his collection of bottles. They were going to have a party even if it was just for two. If he was lucky, Walter would have a few cigars laying around that they could enjoy. He needed to calm down before he went back home.

If Mary wasn't opposed to him keeping a few bottles of his own at home, then he wouldn't have had to leave. But she insisted that they shouldn't have any guns or alcohol in the house because of the kids. At the time, neither was a big concern for him so he gave in without too much resistance. But he saw nothing wrong with having a couple bottles locked up where the kids couldn't get to it in case company dropped by or in case she got on his last nerve like tonight.

"Hey man. What brings you by so late? I was sitting here dozing off," Walter said as he opened his door and fought back a yawn.

"My wife was working my last nerve. I figured I'd come over and have a drink with you." Zachariah entered the house and went straight down to the basement without waiting to be invited. The faster he got a drink, the better. Remembering his manners after he took a sip he inquired, "Why didn't you tell me that you were ready to go to bed when I called?"

"It sounded like something big was going on and you needed to stop by." Walter accepted the drink that Zachariah also poured for him and had a seat. Once he looked comfortable, he continued, "What's going on man?"

"Mary was yelling and screaming because I just told her that I hired a new secretary at the church."

"Is she jealous or something?"

"I don't know. She's been doing that work for me, but now she needs to concentrate on being first lady."

"So when does the lady start working for you?"

"Tomorrow morning."

"Wait a minute. Let me get this straight. You hired a secretary to replace her without telling her that you were looking for someone and the lady starts tomorrow?" That's when the laughter started. Walter almost spit out his drink; he was so amused. "Are you serious? You're lucky all she was doing was yelling." He continued shaking his head and sipping on his drink.

"I don't see how you think this is funny. And why do you always seem to be on my wife's side?" Zachariah asked, puzzled. "She wasn't just yelling. Mary chased me outside in her robe and house shoes."

This made Walter burst into another round of laughter. Zachariah fought back his reflex to join his friend in his amusement. Once he pulled himself together, Walter commented, "Rev, maybe you need to stop drinking hard liquor because I can't understand why you thought she wouldn't be mad. I mean really. You told her the night before the new woman starts to replace her."

"You're right. I shouldn't have put off telling her so long. I'm gonna have to figure out how to get out of the doghouse again."

With that, Walter started cracking up and shaking his head again. His friend definitely didn't look sleepy anymore. While Walter entertained himself being amused about his issues with his wife, Zachariah kept sipping. He thought about it and decided that it was better that he stay away from her for a few hours. She would read her book until she fell asleep and he would ease in the bed next to her. But a few hours later when Zachariah returned home, their bedroom door was locked. He peered over his shoulder and saw that Mary propped a blanket and a single pillow on the couch for him. He sat up straight on the couch fuming for ten minutes. The last time he slept out here, the couch did a number on his back and he woke up as stiff as an ironing board the next day. It would serve her right if she woke up and he was gone. Maybe the next time she disrespected him, he wouldn't bother coming back home at all.

21

"Hi Mrs. Williams. How are you doing?"

"I'm fine. How are you, Erica?"

"I'm hanging in there. I've got a new assistant with me today."

Smiling, Mary spoke to the young twenty-something looking woman behind Erica. "Hello. Come on in." She stepped out of her doorway to allow the two maids to enter the house with their buckets of cleaners, a mop, and vacuum cleaner. Zachariah paid a cleaning service to come once a week to help Mary keep the house spick and span. They scrubbed the bathrooms and kitchen clean. As well as picked up after the kids, dusted, and mopped the floors. She loved the design the vacuum cleaner made on the carpet and wouldn't let anyone cut through the formal dining room, which they never ate in to mess it up.

Mary was never a maid, but she imagined that it must be a grueling job. So she was extra nice and always tipped the women that came to clean. Erica was the lead and had been coming ever since they moved into the house four months ago. Zachariah informed her that she was the same woman that started cleaning his old home once Gloria got too sick to clean. At first Mary didn't like the idea of the same person cleaning for his deceased wife coming to their new home. She thought Erica's allegiance would be with the first Mrs. Williams and would act funny towards her. But Erica was always respectful and sweet to her. Through their weekly conversations, Mary knew that she was in her late forties and had been married for a long time. Erica didn't go to church regularly, so Mary had been trying to entice her to attend service at Mt. Zion by telling her how great the choir sang and how wonderful her husband's sermons were.

An hour after they arrived, Erica had finished cleaning all of the bathrooms and worked her way to the kitchen while her partner was still dusting and vacuuming in the upstairs bedrooms. "Erica, I've got some coffee over there if you want some."

"Thanks, Mrs. Williams. I think I might just pour myself a cup. I could use a boost." As if on cue Erica yawned.

A smirk spread across Mary's face. She imagined

that Erica was tired from staying up late with her husband having fun in bed. "Tell your husband that he can't be keeping you up all night when you have to come here," Mary said between laughs. "That's sweet that y'all are still in love after all these years." Suddenly Mary noticed that Erica didn't respond. A closer look revealed that she was tearing up. "Oh I'm sorry. Did I say something wrong? I was just joking. I didn't mean to offend you."

"No ma'am, you didn't offend me. Actually I've been thinking about finally coming to your church and having your husband pray for me. My husband and I are having a very rough time right now."

"Oh. I'm sorry to hear that." Mary tapped the seat of one of the kitchen chairs so Erica could sit down. But she noticed her hesitate and look over her shoulder towards the stairs. "It's okay. I won't hold you too long," Mary genuinely stated.

Erica gave in and slid down into the seat. She peeked over her shoulder again before she began explaining. "I'm sorry. You must think I'm crazy. I've been crying like a baby all week. And I can't control it. It just comes out of nowhere."

"I'm not trying to be nosey. But you've got to tell me what's going on so I can help you," Mary insisted.

"We've been together since high school." Erica wiped her eye on the sleeve of her uniform so Mary jumped up to get her box of Kleenex for her. She pulled a couple out and wiped her eyes and blew her nose before she continued. "I've been with him for almost twenty-five years. But he's changed. I think he is cheating on me, Mrs. Williams."

Mary exhaled. "What makes you think he's doing something?"

"Most of the time he doesn't answer his cell phone when I call him anymore. He claims he is working late and that he doesn't see any missed calls on his phone."

Mary closed her eyes. For a second Erica sounded like she was talking about Zachariah. She shook her head because from the outside their lives were as different as night and day. Mary was ten years her senior, retired, a newlywed, married to a well-off pastor, and living a life of comfort. Erica was in her forties, doing backbreaking manual labor, had been married over twenty-five years, and spoke a lot about how she and her husband struggled to pay their bills. Yet they were both in unhappy relationships because neither one of their husbands was acting right.

"I found an actress/singer's business card in his wallet."

Mary focused back on their conversation. Her eyebrow raised as she asked, "What were you doing in his wallet?"

Erica shrugged her shoulders and continued her story. "And I found a new credit card in a hidden compartment of the wallet, but I've never seen that bill come to our house. As if that wasn't enough, yesterday I noticed that he wasn't wearing his wedding ring. When I confronted him about it, he claimed that his hand was swollen and the ring was cutting off the circulation in his finger. He had to go out to his car and get it to put it back on." She paused and looked Mary straight in the eyes. "His hand didn't look swollen to me. And at this point, I don't believe anything he says anymore."

"Wow. Did you ask him about her business card or his new credit card?"

"No. If I mention that, then he will know I've been looking through his stuff."

Mary looked up at the ceiling to think and sighed. "That's true."

Both women were quiet for a second. Then Erica broke the silence. "Isn't this where you are supposed to tell me that I'm wrong and my husband loves me and would never do that to me?" Mary's eyes got big and she looked down at the floor. When she finally got the nerve to look up she realized that Erica had a smirk on her face. They shared a quick awkward laugh before she started crying again.

"I'm sorry, honey. I really thought I could help you, but I think you're right. If he doesn't answer his phone, he is somewhere he isn't supposed to be." Almost to herself, Mary mumbled, "Trust me I know." Her maid stared at her curiously. Mary finally sat back down in her chair and blurted out her secret before she changed her mind, "I'm going through some of the same stuff you are going through except my husband is drinking instead of cheating."

Erica tilted her head to the side and glanced over her shoulder making sure her assistant was still in another room. She whispered, "The pastor is drinking?"

Mary's heart started beating out her chest when she realized the huge mistake she just made. She pushed her chair back from the table and stood up. Erica gently touched Mary's arm. "I know my husband isn't the head of a big church like yours is, but your secret is safe with me if my secret is safe with you." Even if she stopped talking, Mary had already confessed what she had kept private from everyone else. So she patted Erica on her hand and sat back down. Erica continued to pour her heart out. "All my friends are divorced or single and looking for a man. Some of them have never even been married. They look at me as being lucky to have a good man. So I can't really talk to them. Besides, my mama once told me that married women have no business taking advice about men from single women unless she wants to be one herself." That brought a grin to Mary's face.

"Have you tried talking to him or asking him if he will go to counseling with you?"

"Mrs. Williams, I've tried talking and the silent treatment. But he has an excuse for everything. That man can come up with a lie quick. Besides he claims that I am delusional and he isn't doing anything wrong. And we can't afford marriage counseling even if I could convince him to go."

Mary shook her head. "So what are you going to do?"

"I was so angry one night when he wasn't home that I started packing all his stuff to put him out. But then I realized that I can't afford all these bills by myself. And if I put him out then whoever he is messing with would take him in. Then she wins and I lose. So I ended up putting everything back where I found it."

Normally, Mary did a much better job of helping someone who was in pain. But at that moment, it was hard for her to give advice considering she needed help with her problems with her husband too. All she could come up with to say was, "We need to keep each other lifted up in prayer. And we need to keep each other updated so we can support one another while we go through this. But I do know that God will make a way. He always does."

They both jumped and turned around when Erica's assistant slammed the vacuum cleaner down a few feet away and began cleaning the living room carpet. She rolled her eyes at Erica sitting down drinking coffee with the client while she was busy cleaning. Erica stood up and yelled over the vacuum, "I'd better get back to work so we can get to our next house. We can finish talking when I come back next time if you want to. But I'm going to try something new. I'm going to pray for you and for me every night until then."

Mary was delighted that she had at least encouraged her enough so that she was going to start praying every day. She stood up too and caught Erica off guard when she embraced her. "I'll be praying for you too."

22

"I love my wife. And I even love her grandkids. But I didn't picture myself raising kids all over again at my age." Zachariah took another sip of his drink.

"Man, that's tough. How old are they again?" Walter asked but never took his eyes off the TV screen directly in front of him across the bar.

"They are sixteen, thirteen, and the little one is eleven. She is a sweetheart, but the other two..." Zachariah didn't finish his sentence.

Acknowledging his friend's concerns, Walter said, "You don't have to tell me. I know how teenagers are. Where are their parents again?"

He took another quick sip of his rum and coke and felt the burn in his throat. "Their dad took off running from the police awhile back. And their mother is on drugs. I agreed to help Mary take care of them because Felicia abandoned them too. But she showed up recently claiming that she is clean. My wife doesn't want to give her back her kids though. She even wants to go to court and fight for them if it comes to that. And of course she wants me to pay for a lawyer to do that."

Walter finally took his eyes off the TV. "What do you want to do?"

"I'm ready for these kids to go back to their mama. For one, they are costing me a fortune. Mary insisted that public schools aren't giving April and Anthony the special attention that they need. And Brooklyn could excel even better at a private school." Zachariah paused for a second. "My kids went to private school so I understand. But that was a long time ago and the tuition is so high now that it's ridiculous."

"How much does tuition cost now?"

"Since it's three of them, we get a family discount. So it's ten thousand a piece."

Walter almost choked on his drink. He caught his breath and hollered, "Did you say a piece?" When Zachariah shook his head Walter stated, "That sounds more like college tuition. Nah, you're a better man than me because they would still be going to public school if I had to pay that much money." He examined his friend up and down and started laughing. "I'm in the wrong line of work. Do you need any help over there at your church Rev.?"

Zachariah briefly shared in his friend's laughter before continuing his rant. "Since my wife died, it was just me. I was lonely and I really liked Mary's company. But now I am not only responsible for Mary, but three more people. And every time I turn around one of them needs something, which means I've got to pay for it since she isn't working. And Christmas is right around the corner. You know how women like to spoil kids during the holidays. I'm scared to look at next month's credit card bill." He took a sip of his drink and continued talking. "Their mama is back now. I know we would have to check up on them to make sure that she hasn't started doing drugs again. But they are her children not mine." He was so worked up that he was talking with his hands as he spoke. "When I get home from a long day at the church, meetings, visiting sick members or having to preach at weddings and funerals, I want to come home and relax. Having these kids to come home to is like having a second job. Mary keeps trying to get me to spend time with Anthony so he will have a father figure. I don't mind helping out, but all that boy really wants to do is play video games and that gets me heated."

"Wow. I wondered why you hung out in this bar all the time. But I see now why you aren't in any rush to go home at night."

"Well I'm glad someone understands what I'm talking about. God knows my wife and I don't see eye to eye on the subject or anything else these days. My first wife wouldn't have given me any problem about sending the kids back to their mother. She always did what I told her to do even if she didn't agree with it."

Walter stared at his friend. "I hope you didn't say something stupid like that to your new wife. Comparing her to another woman is grounds for being cast out of your bed to sleep on the couch if you did."

Zachariah took a big gulp of his drink and didn't answer because that is exactly what had happened when he brought up his beloved deceased wife to Mary. The bar erupted when the Atlanta Falcons scored another touchdown, so he turned his attention to the TV without admitting that he had made that mistake.

Walter pounded the bar. "Man, you've got me over here missing the game."

Truthfully, Zachariah didn't see what was so wrong with letting Mary know what he expected from her. Ephesians 5:22 clearly states that a wife should submit to her husband because he is the head of his wife. How would it look if word got out that he couldn't even control what went on in his own house?

The longer he sat at the bar thinking about their current situation, the angrier he became. *Wasn't he being a provider by being the one paying all the bills? Didn't he move out of his house for her and put her in a house that was better than any home she had ever lived in? Isn't she driving the car she has always dreamed of owning because of him? Wasn't she enjoying going shopping whenever she pleased with the credit card that he gave her? Weren't the kids receiving the best education they have ever received?* He even assured her that he would continue to pay for their tuition once they were back with Felicia. So why couldn't they go home? Was it wrong for him to want his new wife all to himself? She always put the needs of the children before his needs even though The Bible said God comes first and then your husband before anything else. But he didn't feel like preaching to his friend. He decided to stop talking about his personal problems so they could enjoy their drinks and watch the football game in peace.

Part Three

Who in the Hell Left the Gate Open?

23

Mary shot straight up in the bed. Her polyester pajama top was drenched and sticking to her like she had been caught in a rainstorm. She reached for the box of tissue on her nightstand to wipe off her forehead and the back of her neck. Zachariah had been coming home so often at one or two in the morning that she hadn't slept through the night in months. The fact that she had started having hot flashes didn't help her sleep either. Maybe she would call her doctor's office to speak to her about it tomorrow. She focused her eyes to look at the alarm clock and it read two AM. Turning to the other side of their bed, she saw that he wasn't home yet. She got up to use the bathroom, applied a cool washcloth to her neck, and waited for his arrival.

Thirty minutes later, her husband hadn't opened the garage door so she called him. It was no big surprise that his cell phone went straight to voicemail. Instead of answering her call he would let it go to voicemail. Normally, he'd eventually call her back and reply, "Don't be mad. I'm on my way home now, baby" or "Had to make a quick stop. Be home soon" or "Do you need me to pick up something from the store?" The music or noise in the background was always his excuse for claiming he couldn't hear her and rushing off the phone. This time there was no reply at all and that worried her tremendously.

She wondered what a married man was doing out in the middle of the night that was so important that he couldn't answer the phone for his wife. But she didn't like all the ideas that came to her head. Mary was very aware that there were several single women at Mt. Zion that would love to take her place. Her worst fear was that there wasn't really a new friend named Walter, but a beautiful young woman named Wendy instead. She tried to push the horrifying thoughts out of her head because there wasn't anything she could do right now since he wasn't answering his cell.

The blaring alarm clock woke her up again at six o'clock. Mary didn't even remember falling back to sleep. The last thing she recalled was being nervous about Zachariah not picking up his phone. A quick look over her shoulder showed that she was still the only one that had slept in their bed. Mary hit the alarm ranting, "Oh he has lost his mind. How dare he not bother coming home at all." As she marched up the stairs to wake the kids for their first day back to school after Christmas break, she cursed her husband under her breath. She knew that the kids could tell that something was wrong with her. Mary tried, but she was too upset to fake being patient or talk nicely to them like she usually did in the morning. Praying that they did as instructed and got up to avoid getting yelled at again, she quickly stomped back downstairs.

"Where is Pastor?" Brooklyn innocently inquired when she noticed that her grandparent's bedroom was empty and he didn't emerge from the room to eat breakfast with them.

"He had an early meeting at the church." Mary didn't like the fact that a lie rolled off her tongue so quickly. She was picking up Zachariah's new bad habit. Once the kids were safely off to school she sat down at the kitchen table and dialed his number again. Just like the previous five times she called, it went straight to his voicemail. Mary grunted and hung up without leaving a message. She shook her head and covered her face with her hands. "How can he do this to me? I've been nothing but good to that man," she cried out.

During the next several hours, Mary called the church looking for him a few times. When that didn't work, she called several hospitals in the area in case he suffered another heart attack and the emergency room was slow to notify the family. She was grateful that he wasn't admitted to any of them. But she was worried that she still didn't know the whereabouts of her husband who she hadn't seen since he left the house over twenty-four hours ago. Suddenly, the home phone rang with a collect call from him. "What's going on?"

"Baby, I need you to come get me."

"Where are you?"

"I'm in jail. They say I failed a Breathalyzer test."

"Oh my God. You're kidding me right?"

"Baby, I wasn't drunk. I swear. There must have been something wrong with the machine." Mary couldn't help but break down in tears. "Mary, stop crying baby. Don't worry, I'm going to straighten this whole thing out. I just need you to pull yourself together and bail me out of here."

Mary did as instructed and used the credit card that he had given her for household expenses to get a cash advance and bailed Zachariah out of jail. She impatiently waited in the hard chairs for him to be released. It reminded her of the time he gave her the money to get Felicia out of jail. Shaking her head, she reasoned that she was spending way too much time bailing her family members out of bad situations.

Finally, a few hours later, the door opened and there he was. Her normally talkative husband was quiet as he stood near her and waited for her to gather herself. After placing the colorful bookmark that Brooklyn made for her in Art class in between the pages of her book, she took a quick gulp of her black coffee and stood up. There was no desire to kiss the offensive smelling man in front of her. Although Mary usually kept the heat in her Jag on full blast, she decided that they would be riding with the windows down so she could get some fresh air and avoid being knocked out by his funk. In addition to him smelling like a mix of pee and throw up, Zachariah looked very disheveled. His eyes were bloodshot red like he didn't get any sleep yet his short afro was flat on one side like he'd been leaning up against a wall. He didn't seem to care that one side of his button-down shirt was tucked in his dress pants while the other side was hanging out. And his black leather shoes had remnants of vomit splattered on them. For the first time ever, Mary was embarrassed to be seen with her usually very handsome and well put together husband.

When Mary entered the building a couple hours ago, she saw a TV news van parked at the curb but didn't think anything about it. As they exited the building several familiar looking television news reporters approached them blocking their path to her car. They surrounded the couple yelling out questions.

"Pastor Williams, what's your congregation going to say about your DUI arrest?"

"Are you going to resign as senior pastor of Mt. Zion?"

"Reverend, do you have a hangover from Saturday night when you preach to thousands at your church on Sunday mornings?"

Mary was so taken aback that she couldn't move. Zachariah had to grab her by the arm as they maneuvered their way around the journalists. Her instinct was to pull away from him. But she resisted that urge and let him lead her away from the media circus until she realized that he was going down the wrong aisle. In their haste to make a quick getaway it didn't occur to either of them that Mary drove and he had no idea where she parked. She quickly led them two rows over to the safety of her car.

Mary's hand trembled as she tried to put her key in the ignition. Taking a deep breath in, she slowly exhaled to gain her composure before driving off. She was so shocked that word had already gotten out about his arrest. Now both of their faces would be displayed on all the local news stations today. They drove out of the parking lot and down the street in complete silence. Unable to hold her composure any longer she yelled, "You see? You see what I mean? This is exactly what I was afraid would happen. You are going to destroy everything that it took you a lifetime to build. And for what Zachariah? A few drinks?"

"Not now Mary."

"Well my face is going to be on the news now too."

Zachariah belted out, "I said not now. So shut up!"

Her husband had never yelled at her like that before. She had half a mind to slam on the brakes and leave him standing right there on the curb. Instead she yelled back, "Are you still drunk? Don't you ever talk to me like that again."

Mary was so angry that tears welled up in her eyes and she could feel her heart beating faster. Then she heard him say, "Slow down. They aren't behind us." She thought *he must be crazy to speak to me like that and still be talking to me.* But then her eyes checked the gauge and she realized that her lead foot had her doing fifty-five in a thirty-five miles per hour zone. The last thing they needed right now was for her to be pulled over and get a speeding ticket, so she complied and placed her foot on the brake to slow down.

Out of the corner of her eye she could see Zachariah turn his phone on and make a call. "Mr. Parker, this is Zachariah Williams. I'm in a bit of trouble and I need your assistance. Can you call me back on my cell phone as soon as you get this message? Thanks."

Mary knew that Mr. Parker was an attorney. He took care of any legal documents or issues that Mt. Zion had. But she had never heard her husband address him so formally. *He must really be scared. Good. He should be terrified.*

He ended the call and then he called Donald. "Hey. We've got a problem. I need you to make your way over to my house before six." He repeated the same instructions to his sons Joshua and David. Mary shook her head. He was circling the wagons trying to prepare for the trouble that was coming his way. If he had only listened to her, he wouldn't be in this mess.

For the remainder of the ride home, Zachariah didn't speak to her again. He made his phone calls quickly telling the men that he would explain everything in person. Then he looked out the window. Stopped at a red light, she stared at the back of his head and gripped the steering wheel. Had she been thirty years younger in this situation with no kids involved, she would have left him in a heartbeat. Mary was fortunate enough to be able to retire early and she didn't want to have to go back to punching a clock. She was a widow on her second marriage with a house full of grandkids in private school. Her husband paid all the bills and took care of all of them very well. Their life would be nearly perfect if only he wasn't in denial about being an alcoholic.

All she was trying to do was help him but he was shutting her out like he always did when she mentioned his drinking. At this point she had attempted everything over the last four or five months. She tried to talk to Zachariah about his problem, but when he wouldn't talk she gave him the silent treatment. Some nights, Mary acted like she was asleep when he came in the house, other nights she confronted him at the door. When nothing she did worked, she asked David to talk to his dad about his drinking and her husband yelled at her like she was a child in trouble when he came home for worrying his son for no reason. She even asked him to go to marriage counseling with her, but he refused to go.

Once she pulled up the driveway and stopped, Mary noticed how quickly her husband moved. He opened the door and hopped out of the passenger seat of her car before she could put it in park. By the time she made it into the house, she heard water running in the master bathroom shower. "Hmph. He must be in a hurry to wash off his jailhouse dirt." The kids were home from school, and she was thankful that they were in the basement so they didn't see his condition when he came in.

An hour later, Mary was fixing the men hamburgers and French fries for dinner while keeping an eye on the television in the next room. It was rare that they were summoned to the pastor's home instead of the church. So Joshua, David, and Donald had each arrived one after the other right before six. They positioned themselves on the living room sectional with him to watch the evening news. Zachariah had another station's news playing in the corner of the screen using the picture-in-picture feature. The news had been on for a few minutes but so far neither station had mentioned anything about him. That is when she heard, "Up next a well-known local pastor was arrested and faces serious DUI charges." A horrible mugshot of Zachariah popped up on the screen for a couple seconds and then disappeared. Anchor Amanda Davis announced, "That story and more when CBS 46 Atlanta returns."

Mary immediately turned her attention to Zachariah just in time to see his head drop. She almost felt sorry for him for a few seconds. Not only could the media show them leaving the jail repeatedly, but they also had his mugshot to keep broadcasting. Could this get any worse?

She had been told that an alcoholic wouldn't change until they hit rock bottom. Losing his beloved Mt. Zion would be his worst nightmare. While she didn't want that for her spouse, Mary needed something to shake him up and make him see that not only was he messing up his career, but he was destroying their family. A few seconds later, his cell phone rang. He looked at the screen and quickly answered it. "Hello. Yes, I saw it. That's why I've been trying to get in touch with you." Then there was a pause. "Okay. We'll be right here at my house waiting for you to get here."

"Who was that?" David asked.

"That was Paul Parker. He saw the news and is on his way over here to counsel me on what to do next."

24

Everyone got quiet when the news came back on. This time they showed Mary and him walking out of the jail from earlier that day. "Pastor Zachariah Williams of Mt. Zion Baptist Church can be seen here leaving the Fulton County Jail earlier today. He was arrested late last night after police say he failed a Breathalyzer test. CBS 46's Brenda Woods is live in Fulton County with the very latest for us."

The broadcast switched to the reporter filming live in front of the jail. "That's right Amanda. The esteemed pastor and his wife had no comment earlier today when we questioned him about his DUI charges. But CSB 46 will keep you updated on this breaking story. Reporting live outside Fulton County Jail, I'm Brenda Woods for CBS 46 news."

Joshua muted the TV when Amanda came back on the screen reporting on another developing story. Everyone stared at Zachariah.

"Dad, what is going on?"

"This is crazy," David added.

Zachariah stood up and yelled, "This is all a big misunderstanding. The police pulled me over for no reason." He paused and then shouted even louder, "No I'll tell you why they pulled me over. Because I'm a Black man in America who was driving a forty-thousand-dollar Mercedes Benz at two o'clock in the morning and that cop probably can only afford to buy a Yugo."

Mary chimed in and yelled out, "This wouldn't have happened if you weren't running the streets in the middle of the night. You should have been home like every other married man who loves and respects his wife was."

Zachariah saw Joshua grimace and heard David clear his throat. They both jumped a little when he bellowed, "Not now Mary."

The men were trying to ignore the exchange between the couple until Mary slammed a pot on the marble kitchen counter yelling, "Who are you yelling at? I'm only speaking the truth. You need to admit that you have a drinking problem." All eyes were on Mary now. She looked away from her husband and turned to her stepson. "I betcha David was at home with his wife and baby instead of out drinking himself half to death. Weren't you David?"

Zachariah had enough of her. He started moving towards Mary. Donald was the first one to jump to his feet and block his pathway. "What was the reason the officer gave you for pulling you over?"

"Huh?"

The assistant pastor repeated his question to his pastor so his attention would turn away from Mary. Zachariah stopped walking and put his hand to his head. "He said that I ran a stop sign. But I didn't. So he didn't have any reason to pull me over. And I had a couple drinks, but I wasn't drunk."

Mary let out a loud exhale from the kitchen that the men acted as if they didn't hear.

"He probably knew who I was and was trying to make a name for himself in his department. Don't worry, Paul will tell me the best way to fight this."

"Umph umph umph." Mary shook her head and walked to the other side of the kitchen far away from him.

Less than an hour later the men had eaten dinner and were still sitting around waiting for Paul to arrive. Since he hadn't eaten any of the food offered to him in jail, Zachariah was starving. The kids came into the kitchen to grab their plates and say hello to their guests. But he was grateful that Mary let the kids eat dinner downstairs out of their way. He couldn't tolerate any of their foolish bickering right now.

Just as Zachariah checked his watch for the hundredth time, the doorbell rang. He jumped up and let his lawyer in. As he walked back into the room with his family, he stared at Mary. She had embarrassed him enough in front of his sons and his assistant pastor. The last thing he needed was for her to keep making snide remarks about him while Paul was there. When Mary looked up into his eyes he swung his head to the side to motion for her to leave the room. She raised her eyebrow but didn't move an inch, so he spoke up. "Mary, why don't you give us men some time to figure out what to do?" Once again all eyes were on the only female in the room. She apparently decided that going up against him right now was pointless. So she retreated to their bedroom making sure that she slammed the door behind her unnecessarily. He knew she was still close enough to eavesdrop on their conversation, but at least she was out of sight and he wouldn't have to hear her comments.

Zachariah began telling the men in detail how he had stopped at the restaurant to hang out with his friend Walter and have a couple drinks. He stayed until the bar closed at one A.M. Looking at the master bedroom door to make sure it was closed, Zachariah lowered his voice when he admitted to sitting in the parking lot with Walter to drink a couple beers before going home. Joshua and David exchanged glances, but Zachariah kept going because he needed to hear what Paul thought. He would confer with his sons privately later. "Then I rinsed my mouth out with mouthwash so Mary wouldn't say that she smelled alcohol on my breath again. I was on my way home and the next thing I know I see flashing lights in my rearview mirror. I give him my license, registration, proof of insurance and he goes back to his car. He comes back and makes me get out of the car and asks me where I'm going and how much I've been drinking. Then a second patrol car pulls up behind him. They ask me to recite the alphabet backwards, keep touching my nose, and walk a straight line. I can't even do all that stuff when I haven't been drinking." He looked to Joshua for some backup. "Can you say the alphabet in reverse?"

His lawyer interrupted him to keep him on track. "What happened next?"

"One officer says that if I pass the Breathalyzer test they will let me go home." He put his head down and paused. "They said if I refused that I would be charged with a DUI. So I took my chances. I guess I made a mistake. But like I said, they didn't have a reason to stop me in the first place."

The men listened attentively to Paul's advice. "First thing I need you to do is to stop drinking. I don't even want you looking at communion wine." Zachariah smiled until he realized that Paul wasn't grinning back. "I'm serious. And until I tell you otherwise, stay home unless you are at the church or handling church business. Even then I recommended that you stop driving. Every cop in the city will be waiting to pull you over. You make enough money to hire someone that can do security and drive for you. But whatever you do, don't comment about your charges to anyone else."

When their lawyer stopped speaking Donald asked, "How do you plan on winning this case?"

"First, I'm going to request the video from the arresting officer's vehicle to see if he really had probable cause to pull Pastor Williams over. The main thing I'm going to work on is disputing the Breathalyzer findings. I plan to say that the mouthwash you used contained a high percentage of alcohol, which is what was detected on the test. Most officers forget to have their machines regularly calibrated so I hope that is the case with the machine they used on you." Paul looked at his client to make sure that he was satisfied with his answers to the assistant pastor's question. "I've got a ten-page client intake questionnaire that I need you to fill out and get back to me as soon as possible." Zachariah glanced at the forms and agreed to return them quickly. Then he handed Paul a check to retain his services that he prepared while he waited for his arrival.

A few minutes later, Donald walked out when Paul did. Zachariah wished that both his sons saw fit to leave when they did. He knew that they were disappointed in his behavior by the way they looked at him. They wanted answers that he wasn't fully prepared to give them yet.

Joshua spoke up first before his father could even make it back to his spot on the couch. "Dad, have you really been drinking as much as Mary says you have? She says that you stop at a bar and have drinks with your friend a few times a week. And that you stay out until the middle of the night."

"Son, Mary is very upset with me right now. You can't believe everything that she says." He sat down and threw his hands up in the air. "She exaggerates."

Joshua cocked his head to the side and asked, "About which part?"

"All of it." Zachariah looked back and forth between the faces of his sons like he was at a tennis match trying to detect whether or not they believed him. At the same time Joshua paused and looked at David to see if he had any questions. David reacted too slowly, so he continued.

"Well it had to be some truth to it Dad. I mean, you did admit to being out drinking at a bar and sitting outside drinking in a car. And let's not forget that you failed the Breathalyzer test."

Their father quickly objected, "I was at a restaurant not a bar. And you heard what Paul said. It was the alcohol in the mouthwash that made me fail the test. I had a little to drink but I wasn't drunk."

David finally chimed in. "Dad, why didn't you just call a cab to come pick you up?"

"Look," Zachariah yelled, "I'm a grown man and very capable of getting my own self home. I didn't need to call anyone."

David's eyebrows raised and he stared back at him with his mouth open. He turned to look at Joshua who appeared just as speechless. By the way his sons looked at each other, Zachariah realized for the first time that they might actually believe that their stepmother was right, he was in denial and had a drinking problem. They'd known him all their lives. How could they believe that about him? Just because he had one bad night didn't make him an alcoholic.

It wasn't long before Joshua made the excuse that he had to leave to get back to his supper club. Apparently, David didn't want to be left alone with him, so he explained that he needed to get home to his family. Zachariah was left sitting alone in his living room with nothing but his thoughts.

25

"Oh my God. Wow!"

Michael rushed back into Felicia's small living room and stood right in front of her TV. He stared at her with her mouth wide open sitting in a daze. "What happened? What's wrong?" he kept asking.

Felicia shooed him away from blocking her view and grabbed the remote to turn the volume up on the TV. She watched the breaking story about Pastor Zachariah Williams' arrest for DUI on one station until it ended and then quickly changed the channel to another broadcast. It was only when commercials were on all three major local channels that Felicia finally acknowledged Michael. She pointed to the television screen and announced, "That was my mom's new husband, Pastor Williams."

His eyes widened and he broke out smiling. "I've heard of ministers being accused of stealing money from the church, having affairs with the women there, and priests even being accused of messing with underage teenage boys, but this is a new one for me. Drunk driving? A pastor? I didn't even know they were allowed to drink like everyone else."

Felicia stood up with her back to the TV in front of Michael. "My mama acts like she had to check with him about me seeing my kids because I used to do drugs. But he is over there drinking up a storm in front of my kids." She began pacing the floor. "See I knew church folk weren't nothing but a bunch of phonies. My momma used to drag me to his church every Sunday. But my daddy didn't go to church. I wanted to stay home with him. I'll never forget when I asked my momma, "How come I have to go to church, but Daddy gets to stay home in bed?"

She said, "I've tried to get him to come to church with us, but ultimately people are responsible for saving their own souls."

I got smart with her and asked, "Well why can't I be responsible and save my soul later and go back to bed now?"

"What did she say," Michael asked.

"She popped me in my mouth and told me that adults were responsible for themselves. Since I was a child she was responsible for me. But I know the church is full of hypocrites. Her own husband is the ringleader and he is the biggest one. That's why I don't waste my time going anymore."

Michael stood up and blocked her path. "Okay baby. Calm down." He lifted her face so that she was looking up at him.

She exhaled and rested her head on his muscular chest. "I can't believe that I let them make me feel like I wasn't good enough for my own kids anymore because they've got that huge house, fancy cars, and all that money. My kids are in private school now, something that I would never be able to afford." Felicia let go of Michael's back and pulled away from his embrace. "But behind closed doors the fine upstanding pastor ain't nothing but a drunk. And that's the man my kids are living in that house with and looking up to?"

Felicia started pacing the floor again. This time she walked behind the couch so her boyfriend wouldn't stop her. He wanted her to calm down but she didn't want to. She had been patient and moving too slowly to get her kids back as it was. But when April informed her that she didn't want to come back home, Felicia felt more hurt than she wanted to admit. Her plan was to spend time with her kids and show them that she had changed hoping that they would willingly come home. However, this incident with Pastor gave her every reason in the world to speed up the process.

"I'm going to get my kids back."

"That's right. Nobody is going to stop you from getting your kids back," he agreed with her. "Baby, I already told you that I could help you get a bigger place. I don't know why you won't let me help you out."

"I don't need your help," she yelled much louder than she intended to. Immediately she realized how rude she was being. But he was always trying to help her to the point where it was a little irritating. If she had met him at another time in her life when she was impressed with all the trappings that a man could provide for her, she would take him up on his offer. Michael was a good guy. But she got the impression that he liked her a lot more than she liked him and she didn't want to use him. Staying off drugs, working hard for tips, and getting her kids back were the only things she was focusing on these days.

"I'm sorry baby I didn't mean it like that." Felicia walked back over to him and gently touched his chest. "I already told you, when Anthony Sr. left us I didn't have anything. No college education, no work experience, no money, no nothing. He promised to take care of me and the kids forever and I believed him." Michael looked like he was about to interrupt her. "Before you say it, I know that you aren't like him. But I just need to prove to myself that I don't need a man to take care of me or my kids. I can do it all by myself."

Michael threw his hands up in surrender. "Okay. I hear you."

A couple hours later, Felicia anxiously picked up her phone and dialed her mother's number. Immediately her mother gave her attitude. "This isn't a good time right now Felicia. Let me call you back tomorrow."

"No, don't hang up this phone, Ma." She could hear her mother breathing heavily on the other end. "I saw you on the news earlier."

"Chile, I said I don't have time for this right now."

"You've got my kids over there with an alcoholic so you'd better hear what I have to say." Once again her mother listened to her command without any objection. Felicia wasn't one hundred percent sure before, but now realized that her mother was scared. If there was no truth to the accusation against her husband, her mother would have easily gotten off the phone with no regard for what Felicia was saying. That fact that her mother let her be stern with her spoke volumes. So she took hold of the power that she had. "I'm coming to pick up my kids Friday after school. And they are going to spend the weekend with me." The other end of the phone remained quiet. "I'll bring them back Sunday evening after dinner."

"Fine. I'll make sure that they are ready to go when you get here."

"Also, we need to have a serious conversation about my kids moving back in with me."

"I think we should at least wait until the end of the school year before we consider something that drastic."

"They are my kids and I don't want to wait that long. I'm working on getting a bigger place for us now.

The longer they stay with you, the harder the transition will be," Felicia insisted. "Anyway, we don't need to talk about that today. I know that you are dealing with something else right now. But I do want to have that conversation very soon."

"See you Friday," her mother said, hanging up before Felicia could respond.

26

"Everybody come sit down. I need to talk to you." Once April, Jr., and Brooklyn sat down at the kitchen table, Mary started one of the hardest conversations of her life. "Your mother is going to fight me to regain back custody of you three."

April was the first to speak up. "Do you think a judge would really make us live with her again even though she does drugs?"

"I think your mother is telling the truth this time about not doing drugs anymore."

Her oldest grandchild's eyes suddenly lit up

anyway. "My friend Robin's parents got divorced and she said since she was over fourteen, the judge asked her who she wanted to live with. So when they ask me, I'll just tell them that I want to stay here with you."

Mary bit her bottom lip. "I don't know if it's going to be that easy. Besides, what about your brother and sister? They aren't over fourteen."

April shrunk back down in her chair deflated. She mumbled, "I'm not going back. I don't care what anyone says."

Mary examined her other grandchildren. Anthony was staring off into the distance and Brooklyn was eyeballing her big sister like she didn't know what to say. Her silence made Mary wonder if Brooklyn wanted to live with her mother again, but didn't want to hurt her feelings.

Before Mary could ask her, April interrupted her thoughts. "Can she even take care of us? She said that she is a waitress. How much do waitresses make? Whatever it is, I know it won't be as much as you and Pastor."

What a difference a year has made. When Mary knocked on their apartment door to pick up the kids, April was so defiant. Mary thought that she was going to have to call for help to come drag April out of there kicking and screaming to make her leave. Now she was determined to stay with her no matter what.

"That's true, but she is your mother. And if she is off drugs and has a clean, safe place for you to live, then you may have to go." Mary groaned and closed her eyes.

"Plus this DUI situation with Pastor is going to look bad to a judge."

Finally, Brooklyn spoke up. "What does DUI mean, Grandma?"

"It means he got in trouble for drinking alcohol and then getting in his car and driving." Mary thought that was the simplest way to explain it.

April chimed back in, "Can't he fight it? Robin says that if you have money and a good lawyer you can get out of anything, even murder. He didn't hurt anyone and he has money so won't he win?"

This situation wasn't funny, but Mary grinned. "Your friend Robin seems to know a lot about court, huh?"

April shrugged. "Her mom told her that people are always suing her daddy, but he always wins because he has a great lawyer and a lot of money. When the other people run out of money, they give up so he wins."

Mary folded one arm across her chest and rubbed her chin with the other hand. "I guess Mr. Parker, the church's lawyer, can represent us. He's a great attorney according to Pastor." But before she asked him to represent her, she needed to ask them what they really wanted. Since Anthony was still quiet Mary began with him first. "Jr., do you want to stay here or do you want to move back in with your mother? I want you to be honest with me. I won't be mad at you no matter what you decide. So if you want to go back with your mom you can tell me."

Anthony looked up after a few seconds. "Umm. I want to stay here."

Mary silently exhaled and turned to her youngest grandbaby. "What about you Brooklyn?"

"I don't want anyone to be mad at me," she answered and started sobbing. April reached out and rubbed her little sister's back, Mary grabbed Brooklyn's hand and smiled at her.

"Nobody is going to be angry at you, baby. I promise. So are you saying that you want to go back and live with your mommy?" Mary braced herself for her answer.

Brooklyn wiped the tears away that were running down her cheek. "Why can't Mommy move in with us? We've got plenty of room here?"

Mary suddenly began coughing. Brooklyn's question caught her totally off guard and almost made her choke. Through her watery eyes, she could see April shaking her head and laughing at her little sister. When Mary finally caught her breath she answered. "Your mother is a grown woman. She doesn't want to come live with her mother again."

"Stupid little girl."

"That's enough Anthony," Mary yelled.

Everyone at the table was staring at Brooklyn waiting for her to give another answer to the question. She finally said, "I want to stay here with everyone else, but I want to be with my mom too. I don't want to hurt Mommy's feelings. If we don't go back, she will be all by herself."

This was a nightmare. No matter who won the fight, her grandbabies would be the ones to get hurt. They were already hurting from their dad leaving and mother not being around consistently. Mary's biggest fear was what if they moved back in with Felicia and she forbade her from calling or coming around like she did before. No matter how much her grandkids worried her or misbehaved at times, Mary couldn't bear to be without them again. Living with each other made them closer than they had ever been before. So if Felicia wanted a fight, a fight is what she was going to get.

27

Their ride to church was quieter than any other time
Zachariah had been in the car with Mary and the kids.
Maybe it was because he was riding in the back with April,
Anthony, and Brooklyn. Once he got his car from the
impound, he listened to his lawyer's advice and
immediately hired a big man who came highly
recommended to be his driver/bodyguard. Chuck was
driving his Mercedes while Mary sat next to him in the
passenger seat.

Zachariah knew that it was going to be a long,
difficult day. Today he was going to have to stand before
his congregation at both services knowing that most, if not

all, of them had heard about his recent DUI charge. So he asked Mary and the kids to ride with him and attend both services. He wanted them to appear to be a united front even if they weren't. Mary was barely speaking to him these days. So much for having a supportive wife. Zachariah was so grateful that his assistant pastor had convinced him to hire a secretary before all of this started. The less time he had to spend with his wife during these tense times the better.

Suddenly Mary opened up his glove compartment, they hit a bump, and his Lagerfeld cologne, travel size bottle of mouthwash, and a flask tumbled out. She pulled on her seatbelt to loosen its restraints so she could lean forward and pick them up. Holding them in her hand, she examined the items for a few seconds before turning to him. "Why in the world are you riding around with a flask in your car?"

"What are you doing going through my stuff?" he fired back from the back seat.

"I was looking for the Kleenex I put in here before to wipe my forehead." She answered without taking her eyes off her husband. "Stop changing the subject and answer my question. Why do you have this," she shook the flask in her hand, "in your car?"

"Let's talk about this later when we are alone, Mary."

Mary looked over her shoulder at the three kids in the back and reluctantly gave in to his suggestion to finish their heated discussion later. *Why do I have to answer to her about what I keep in my glove compartment anyway?* It was his car. It's not like she found a condom or a pair of lady's underwear in there. Chuck's foot must have gotten heavy due to their argument because in no time they were pulling up in front of the church.

When Mary climbed out of his Benz she couldn't let the argument go. She looked up at their billboard across the lot and shook her head. "Umph umph umph. What a joke." Then she shot Zachariah a dirty look. He looked around to make sure that no one had seen her outburst, but it was still early. Aside from a handful of cars, one of which was David's, the lot was practically empty. Zachariah arrived early on purpose to avoid his members until it was time to walk up to the pulpit. "Come on y'all, let's go inside," she said to the children only.

Pausing to stare at the billboard himself, Zachariah remembered the day Mary and he took that picture. They were still engaged at the time and she was excited about the billboard being unveiled on their wedding day for all the congregation and wedding guests to see. She lovingly picked out outfits for them to wear days before the shot and couldn't contain her excitement about it. He remembers Mary being thrilled that the same ladies hired to do her hair and makeup for their wedding day, were also available to do them for the photo shoot. Zachariah realized how much things had changed for the worse in the last several months. He grinned at how beautiful his wife's smile was and hoped that she would paint it on today in front of the congregation. He felt a cool breeze whipping against his face and decided to get inside.

Expecting to see his family in his office when he opened the door, Zachariah was a little disappointed when they weren't there waiting for him. So he set out to find them. He discovered April in the music room with David rehearsing a solo while Brooklyn tried on a choir robe that was ten times too large for her. Anthony sat behind the drum set pretending to play them while his sister sang. Zachariah waved to his son, but turned to go so he wouldn't disturb them.

After checking the sanctuary and several other rooms, he finally found Mary down in the church kitchen with an apron on helping prepare the food that was sold by the plate after each service on Sundays. Cooking always calmed Mary down. That should have been the first place he looked for her. Instead of asking her to join him upstairs, Zachariah backed out of there before any of the ladies noticed him. He wasn't sure what would be worse, his wife making up an excuse not to follow him upstairs and embarrassing him in front of a kitchen full of nosey women, or her coming upstairs and then continuing their argument about his flask.

He returned to his office busying himself by going over what he was preparing to say to his congregation for what must have been the hundredth time. But he still wasn't sure of the right words to say. All he knew was that he couldn't have his members doubting his innocence and believing the lies being spread by the media the last several days. He had half a mind to sue them for slander. For that matter, he wanted to sue the police officers for false arrest as well. Sure he had a few drinks, but he was in no way drunk. It took a lot more than a few drinks to get him drunk. *Did it really take more than a few drinks to get him drunk these days?* Sitting in the house of the Lord, he had to admit to himself that it did. But he waved the negative thoughts away and convinced himself that his wife was such a great cook that he had been steadily gaining weight since they married. All of his pants were a little snug now. The added pounds must be the reason that it took more to get him intoxicated now.

Zachariah finally started to hear lots of movement in the building. This meant that it would be time for him to face his congregation soon. He was still studying his notes when he heard a knock on the door. "Come in."

Joshua walked in and exhaled. "Hey Dad," Joshua said without so much as a fake smile on his face as he entered and closed the door.

Zachariah overlooked his dryness. He was just happy that his firstborn was there. Ever since he opened the supper club his regular attendance at Zion had waned. The family never knew if he was going to show up or not. Zachariah got up from behind his desk to hug him. "Hey son. I'm glad you could make it. We haven't seen you here a lot lately."

"It's hard getting up early when you've been up all night working," he answered as he plopped down in the nearest chair. "I still pray and read my Bible though."

Not wanting to alienate Joshua, Zachariah didn't pry any further. "Well, I'm glad that you made it today. I need all the support I can get." He moved back behind his desk.

Joshua looked around and asked, "Where's Mary?"

"Last I checked she was helping the ladies cook in the kitchen." Zachariah looked down. "I asked her to come support me, but she is still upset. So I'm not sure why I even bothered. There is so much tension around my house right now."

Joshua leaned back in his chair. "How is she acting when she is here?"

Zachariah realized that Joshua didn't know yet. "That's right, you haven't been here. I hired a full-time secretary, so Mary doesn't need to be here all the time."

His son sized him up and leaned forward again finally showing some emotion for the first time. "You mean Mary was okay with you hiring someone?"

Shrugging his shoulders, he replied, "No. She wasn't okay with it at first. But she really didn't have much of a choice. It was my decision to make." Zachariah threw his hand up in the air. "She is probably delighted that she doesn't have to see me that much anymore now."

"Is she still acting like she did the other night at the house?"

Zachariah had one word to say. "Worse."

Joshua slid back in the chair. "Well Dad, can you blame her?"

Zachariah was shocked that his son was on his wife's side. It wasn't that long ago that Joshua was against him dating and then marrying her. And now he was sitting in his office defending her over his own father. "Look, I'm happy that you are here. But I don't have time for this right now."

"I'm just saying that you've only been married a few months. So far you've left her in Jamaica alone on your honeymoon, you've been hanging out in bars, and now you have a DUI. I wouldn't be happy with you if I was her either."

There was another knock on the door interrupting them. But this time they didn't wait to be invited in. Donald stuck his head in and announced, "It's time Pastor."

28

"I want you to know that no matter what you may hear in the news, the DUI charge against me is false and I'm going to do everything in my power to fight it." There were outbursts of applause. Then it got quiet again so the congregation could hear what else he had to say.

Mary sat in her usual spot on the first pew of the church dressed in a green paisley print dress and black heels. Brooklyn and Anthony sat quietly next to her dressed in their Sunday best as well. Listening to her husband pound on the pulpit vehemently denying the case against him had her stomach doing flips. If he went on for much longer, she was going to have to excuse herself to go use the restroom. But if she went out the sanctuary door, she couldn't promise that she would have the strength to come back in and continue listening to her husband.

She was relieved that it sounded like he was finally wrapping up his speech, because Mary also didn't know how much longer she could hide behind the poker face she managed to pull off. When one of the members sitting directly behind her touched her shoulder to comfort her, it did the exact opposite and she nearly lost her composure. Praying that the tears welling up wouldn't betray her and fall, she gripped the tissue that she held in her hand. But she wasn't about to cry out of empathy for her husband's situation. If her tears fell it would be out of sheer embarrassment.

As the first lady of Mt. Zion, Mary apprehensively participated in Zachariah's attempt to show a united family front to the world, but it was all a façade. She was both extremely disappointed and equally furious with him. How could she stand by someone who she didn't believe in anymore? If she wasn't catching him in one lie after another, he was walking around their house not speaking to her at all acting like she was the one in the wrong.

What she knew was that he should have been home that night with his family. Instead he was out drinking with a new friend that she still hadn't met despite Zachariah's word that she would be introduced to Walter. And where was this good friend right now, she wondered? The man who her husband was having so much fun with that he couldn't tear himself away to come home at a decent hour.

Was he sitting in shame on a nearby pew with all eyes fixed on him like they were glued on her? No. Of course not. He got to have all the fun with her husband while she and her grandchildren had to endure the disgrace.

This had to be one of the most humiliating experiences of her entire life. Being the first family of the church, they should have been the upstanding dignified leaders setting the example and advising their members not to get caught up in these types of situations, not defending themselves for being in one. It was easy to hold your head up high when everyone knew that you were raising your grandkids because their mother was on drugs, because Felicia never came to church. And truth be told, there were several other grandmothers in the congregation who had to step up and raise their grandkids for the same reason too. There were a few whispers about it before they married. Now that she was first lady, no one would dare to say anything bad about it to her. But to have to hold your head up standing beside the very man who preaches to them every Sunday about living right when he was the one who wasn't, was a whole 'nother thing. How long was she going to have to endure this shame?

This can't be what being a first lady was all about Mary reasoned. She knew that he would be gone a lot doing church business. The deacons, people in charge of the different ministries, and other people that helped out also had full-time day jobs. So it wasn't out of the ordinary that he would have to meet with them after normal business hours. The members of Mt. Zion were very important to him. And with such a large congregation, it seemed like someone was always in the hospital that needed him to pray over them. But running around handling ministerial issues wasn't what he was doing until the wee hours of the morning. As crazy as it seemed, Mary almost wished that his addiction was with another woman. A rival that was one hundred percent woman, she could handle. She had enough self-confidence that no matter how curvy or cute her opponent was, she could defeat her and win back the attention of her husband. But she had no idea how to compete with a bottle that was forty proof.

Even if her support wasn't wholehearted, from the looks of this crowd, the saints came out in droves to support their pastor. The seats were overflowing with members squeezed into the pews like they used to be when there was only one service and it was Mother's Day. She wondered what they would think if they knew that he really had been drinking and driving and that he did it on a regular basis before this incident. Mary also noticed a bunch of unfamiliar faces as well. Maybe they were just nosy and wanted to witness the pastor who was an alcoholic. Hopefully, none of them were reporters or photographers trying to stir up trouble so they could get a story.

Mary glanced over at Chuck, Zachariah's new driver/bodyguard. He was tall enough to have to bend his head down in doorways and wide enough that he probably needed a seatbelt extension on an airplane. Chuck definitely shopped in the big and tall department, so he couldn't be overlooked. She wondered if anyone here figured out what his job was yet. When she overheard

Zachariah introducing him to the kids, he told them about his credentials. The girls weren't interested one bit, but Jr. asked him if he could show him some Jiu Jitsu moves. From what she could see while still trying to appear busy and uninterested, he was good. But Mary wondered if he could handle more than one person if he had to. She was very upset with Zachariah and his juvenile behavior, but the last thing in the world she wanted was for her husband to get hurt in a commotion.

Mary was in such a daze that it took her a minute to realize that Zachariah had finally stepped back from the podium and taken his seat. April was standing in the pulpit. She tuned in and realized that she had already started singing her song. Her beautiful voice brought a proud smile to Mary's face. God had touched her grandbaby's heart and helped her turn her life around like Mary prayed that He would do. April still occasionally had an attitude and was selfish like most teenagers, but she didn't give her half the problems that she used to. Now all of Mary's prayers were for her wayward husband. Unlike April, she couldn't use his age as an excuse for his bad behavior. He was definitely old enough to know better. And he was too old to start having a midlife crisis.

Mary attempted to quiet her thoughts and enjoyed listening to the choir accompanying April as she sang, "I Know I've Been Changed." She really absorbed the inspiring words that April was now belting out. Normally, Mary remained seated and swayed from side to side or clapped her hands for her favorite songs. But it felt like April knew what she needed and was singing the lyrics directly to her. So after a couple minutes, Mary couldn't help but jump up, throw her hands up in the air and shout, "Hallelujah! Thank you Jesus!"

She had to believe that her family was going through what it was battling against to come out better on the other side. The tears that she held back for so long were now running freely down her face because she didn't care about them anymore. They were falling for a different reason now. She was excited about what was going to come, not for what they were going through. The song was a shocking reminder that she had temporarily lost her trust in God. But it was also a sign that even if we don't know what His plan for us is, He does and He can change any situation. We just have to have faith.

29

Mary grew suspicious when Felicia didn't readily offer the name of the restaurant she worked at to her or her children. Assuming that she was lying about working a legal job, because she never had one, Mary had her followed in case she needed more ammunition to fight to keep her grandbabies from an unfit mother. She almost passed out when the private investigator she hired informed her that Felicia was an employee at a popular Atlanta strip club called Club Stiletto. Nothing her daughter did should surprise her anymore, but it always did. She breathed a sigh of relief when he informed her that she was a waitress there, not a stripper.

At least she still had a little bit of sense and wasn't

lying about having a job waiting tables. Maybe she really was trying to get her life together. Mary felt bad about preparing to go to battle against her only child. But she reasoned that it was Felicia's fault. If she had listened to any of the advice that Mary had given her when she was younger, they wouldn't be in this mess now. She wouldn't have shacked up with Anthony Senior and had three of his kids out of wedlock while solely depending on his drug dealing lifestyle to keep a roof over their heads. If it were up to Mary, her daughter wouldn't have been pregnant during her senior year in high school and given up any chance she had of going to college. Mary suddenly realized what she was thinking. That would mean there wouldn't be an April. And probably no Anthony Jr. or Brooklyn either. She tried to imagine her life without her grandkids but couldn't. The two years that Felicia kept them from her were extremely difficult for her. And she was very grateful to have them back in her day-to-day life.

Mary kept thinking that there had to be another way to go about this. Her older brother and sister laughed at Brooklyn when she suggested that Felicia move in with them. But maybe she was on to something. An innocent child's first instinct had been for her family to come together. Why had Mary's initial reaction been to fight? *If Felicia was drug free and working on herself, then shouldn't she get her kids back? Did they really need to try and make each other look bad and spend thousands of dollars fighting in court making two lawyers rich battling when they both wanted the same thing?* Ultimately, everyone wanted what was best for the kids. And if Mary won, was it good for the kids to be in the house with a man who didn't really want them there anymore? When her husband was around, which wasn't often these days, he seemed less patient with the kids than before. And he had made it clear to Mary that he felt they should be with their mother. She wondered if that would make a difference in her troubled marriage. But what if she sent them back to her daughter and Zachariah still spent all his time away from home. He could be using them as an excuse when he really wanted to be out of the house anyway. Then Mary would end up being in that huge house all alone and miserable with no grandkids and a new husband who was M.I.A.

Zachariah already said that he would still pay the kids' tuition if they moved back in with their mother. She hoped that he wasn't lying and hadn't changed his mind about that. If what he promised were true, then they would still be getting the best possible education no matter where they lived. So maybe this family crisis had happened to get her relationship back with her grandkids and get them to a better school. But it wasn't easy getting April in that school. Grove Wood Academy wanted Brooklyn and even Anthony because his grades had improved tremendously since he moved in with her. At first April's application had been denied while her siblings were accepted.

Mary vividly recalled the conversation that she had with Zachariah about it. "Mary, you knew that it would be a long shot getting April in there in the first place. At least Brooklyn and Anthony got in."

"If they don't want April, then they can't have any

of them," she insisted. "Can't you use your influence to get her in?" When her husband wasn't sure what more he could do to help, she continued ranting. "It's not too late to apply at other schools."

"Baby, do you really want to put the kids through this application process again? I'm sure all the private schools in Atlanta have similar admission guidelines."

After a few more minutes of negotiating, Zachariah agreed to try and pull some strings to get April in. A week later, a letter arrived from the academy informing them that they had reconsidered and decided to admit April as well. She wasn't sure what her husband had done, but whatever it was all three of her grandbabies were headed into a brighter future.

Getting back to the problem at hand, Mary wondered if she could convince Felicia to let the kids stay with her the days she had to work at the club. That way she could still see them several times a week. If they spent the night on Saturday night, then April would still be able to go to church on Sunday and sing in the choir. Surely Felicia wouldn't make her firstborn give up the one thing that brought her joy because she had doubts about God.

Mary was stressed out thinking about all this. She was the first lady of one of the best Baptist churches in Atlanta. But her husband, the pastor, was in denial about having a drinking problem. And if he didn't wake up and get his life together soon, they were going to lose it all. Now she had to deal with her daughter working at a strip club. What if someone found that out too? Atlanta was known for having some of the best strip clubs in the country. Although it might not be a place their regular members frequented, clubs weren't illegal. It was very possible that someone from the church could go there and recognize Felicia. It had been several years since she attended regularly, but she did grow up in the church. How could Mary explain her daughter, the pastor's stepdaughter, working in a filthy environment of nudity and excessive drinking to God-fearing church folks?

She knew that despite all of their problems, God didn't allow the blessings to come into her life for her to lose them all. Mary tried to take her mind off her personal problems by getting back to work on the church's annual women's day event. There was a lot to do in a short period of time. Including replacing one of the first lady headliners who had been confirmed a couple weeks ago. Now that word was getting out nationally about Zachariah's DUI, the out-of-state speaker suddenly had a scheduling conflict and had to cancel. Mary would have respected her more if she had simply called her and honestly admitted that she didn't think she should be associated with them during this ordeal. Instead, the popular first lady who was touring to promote her book on forgiveness of all things, backed out via an email from her assistant. Since it had already been announced that she was coming, Mary was going to have to fill her spot with an even larger personality to save face.

Despite her late start and a few setbacks, Mary was determined that this year's celebration was going to be the best Mt. Zion had ever had. She was following in the footsteps of the late first lady. Mary knew that the church ladies were good at gossiping and would openly compare their events to each other all while patting her on the back and telling her that she did an amazing job.

Her friend Brenda was great at planning events. She took on planning her family reunion every year practically by herself and did a fantastic job with the accommodations, transportation, games, outings, and meals for over a hundred family members. Whenever Brenda had a milestone birthday, she planned memorable themed events. One year, Brenda planned a bucket list party that their book club still raves about 'til this day. She took the name literally and decorated her place with everything from bucket serving dishes for the food they ate to bucket candle holders. The guests spent the day writing their own lists and signing up for items to help Brenda check off her personal bucket list. Mary's personal favorite was the year she threw a white party. Everything from the drinks, plates, linen, decoration, and cake was white. And only two people were disobedient and wore clothing that were not all white. But her friend even thought ahead and bought plain white t-shirts just in case that happened.

Mary wanted to call her for some advice but felt like she couldn't. They hadn't seen or spoken since her birthday fiasco at the mall. Using church business and the kids as excuses for not attending recent monthly book club meetings was Mary's way of avoiding her friend. Her fear was that maybe First Lady Ward was right when she said Brenda was jealous of her. Had she given her reason to be? Perhaps her excitement about all the new things in her life had come off as boasting. She never meant to brag or show off. Mary knew that ultimately everything she had was because of God's favor on her life and she didn't take credit for any of it.

Brenda was too good of a friend to lose because of hurt feelings and any misunderstanding. Mary had some bad things going on in her life too and she missed talking to her friend about them. So she quickly picked up the phone and dialed Brenda's number before she talked herself out of it.

30

When her mother called and asked her to lunch,
Felicia didn't know what to expect. She was always a
daddy's girl because he didn't judge her like her mama did.
For as long as she could remember, everything she did
seemed wrong in her mother's eyes. She was always
fussing about Felicia not doing her chores well enough.
Mary didn't like the way she wore her clothes and said she
put on too much makeup. Her average grades weren't good
enough. She didn't like her high school sweetheart and
wasn't happy any of the times she was pregnant, even
though she was grown and out of her house for the last two.
And most of all, she didn't approve of her decision not to
go to college when she graduated from high school. Felicia
couldn't bear to see the look on her mother's face if she
saw the way her appearance changed once she started doing

drugs. So she stayed away and kept her kids from seeing her too, fearing that they would let her know what was going on in their household.

For the first time in her life, Felicia could finally shake her head and look down her nose at her mother's choices and what had been going on in her mini mansion household. Yes, she was taking care of her kids for her. But she seemed to be married to a man who looked great to the outside world but was a functioning alcoholic, while Felicia was working hard every day around ogling, drunk, and frisky men to be able to get back on her feet and provide for her kids. She was ready for her kids to come back home. So they had a lot to talk about.

Felicia pulled off the interstate and headed up Piedmont Road towards Buckhead. Within a few minutes she was turning left onto Pharr Road. After a minute, she saw the big scaly fish that she was looking for. Her new boyfriend liked simple food like pizza or hot wings and fries, so she hadn't been to a fancy restaurant since Anthony Senior was around. She was looking forward to some seafood and heard that The Atlanta Fish Market had some of the best in town.

Inside she saw her mother sitting down by the entrance patiently waiting for her. The first lady had on an expensive looking new pea green wool jacket, black dress pants, and matching heels. Felicia felt a little underdressed in her jeans. She was relieved that she had at least picked a pretty shirt under her aging leather jacket for their lunch date.

"I'm sorry I'm late, Ma. Traffic was horrible," she explained. Felicia was happy that she was sitting down. It gave her an excuse not to give her an awkward fake hug.

Her mother stood, smiled and said, "It's okay. I got stuck in it too. But you're here now so let's get us a table."

Felicia couldn't wait to order. Her taste buds were craving some jumbo shrimp cocktail as an appetizer and fresh salmon as her entree. She was looking at the vast menu to see how the chef prepared it. When her mother ordered crab cakes, Felicia almost changed her mind and ordered them instead, but she figured that she could talk her mother into giving her one and stuck to the salmon. After they ordered, Felicia took a couple sips of her drink and grew impatient waiting for her mother to get to the reason for this lunch invite.

"So I guess you are wondering why I invited you to lunch with me."

"You must be reading my mind."

"I wanted to talk about the kids."

"What about my kids?" Felicia interrupted. "You said they were okay."

"They are fine and I want them to stay that way."

Felicia rolled her eyes. "They're not staying with you Ma," she announced louder than she meant to. This was so typical of her mother. She always thought she knew what was best for everyone. "I hope you didn't bring me all the way here to try and change my mind about that."

Mary put her hand up to get an opportunity to speak. "I have a compromise that I think is a win-win for everyone involved." Felicia shook her head and sighed. So her mother started talking faster. "What if I fixed up my old house for you and the kids? We could finish off the basement by installing central air, separate the space into two bedrooms, and lay down wall to wall carpet down there." Felicia sat quietly staring at the woman in front of her with her eyebrows raised. "They would be back in the same neighborhood with their friends and you would be back in the house that you grew up in. I know how much you love that house."

Felicia tilted her head to the side and asked, "What's in this for you? Why are you doing this?"

Mary met Felicia's disbelief with a bit of aggression. "Look, I don't want to fight you. I just want to do what's best for the kids."

"You mean my kids," Felicia corrected with an attitude in her voice.

"I know they are your kids. I'm just trying to help." The waiter coming to the table with their appetizer silenced their argument that was about to get heated. By the time he walked away, they had each taken a few deep breaths. Mary took a couple forkfuls of her Caesar salad before continuing. "I'm not up to anything, baby. You know my house is paid for. Of course you would have to put the utilities in your name. You can't stay there for free, but I'm sure we can agree on a fair amount of rent that you could afford."

"Oh I get it. You want us in your house so you can walk in and check on us whenever you want." Before her mother could protest Felicia continued. "I told you that I'm clean. Don't I look clean to you?" Felicia looked around and realized that she was still talking louder than she should be at an upscale restaurant. Embarrassed, she grabbed a shrimp and stuck it in her mouth.

"I know you are clean," Mary insisted. "Do you think I would be willing to help you if you weren't? The house is still in good shape and the people on my old street look out for each other. That's why I stayed for so long."

Still not convinced, Felicia interrupted, "Oh. I thought you stayed because it was down the street from Mt. Zion."

"That too." Mary smiled. "Now the kids will be close to the church again. April can keep singing in the choir. And if you are going to have to work Saturday nights and don't want the kids to stay home, they can stay with us and we can take them to church."

Felicia ate her last shrimp and didn't answer. She wanted to tell her mother no, but if she did it would be out of spite. Living in her old house sounded better than staying in any fifteen hundred square foot apartment that she could barely afford. She knew that her mother's house didn't have rats and roaches, but she wouldn't know what an apartment had until she paid her deposit and moved in.

But if she said yes, then her mother won. She'd never done what her mother wanted her to do before. Why start now?

"I don't know if I want my kids going to a church that has an alcoholic for a leader." Felicia waited for her mother's quick comeback, but she didn't have one. Instead she put her fork down without finishing the last of her salad. Right on cue, their waiter brought their main courses out and cleared away their other plates. "So you don't have nothin' to say?"

"Honestly, I don't know what to say other than it's better to trust in the Lord instead of man." Her mother put her head down for a few seconds before she looked back up. "My husband had a couple of close friends die and it changed him. He isn't the man I've known all these years or even the man I married six months ago. He has a problem and I'm trying to help him work on it." Mary used the napkin to blot the area under her eyes dry and looked around the restaurant.

The miserable expression on her mother's face made Felicia feel sorry for her. As much as they were different, it seemed like they had at least a couple things in common. They both loved April, Anthony Jr., and Brooklyn. It also seemed like they each had their heart broken by men that they believed in. Felicia didn't want to start feeling sad about Anthony Senior so she shoveled a bite of her well-done salmon in her mouth before it started to get cold.

To change the subject Felicia asked, "What about Grove Wood Academy? I think the kids like going there."

That brought the smile back to their grandmother's face. "They do. That's the good thing. Zachariah said that he would keep paying their tuition even if they didn't live with us anymore."

"Really?" Felicia couldn't hide her shock. She made designs in her mashed potatoes with her fork as she thought about their conversation. Finally, she asked, "How long will it take before the house is ready for us to move back in?"

Mary reached across the table and grabbed her other hand. She squeezed it tight with one hand and wiped her tears from her face with her free hand. Felicia knew that this was the first time in a long time that her mother was proud of one of her decisions.

31

April didn't like being a teenager right now. At this awkward age you had the impression that you were close to being a grownup so they should value your opinion, but that was just an illusion. Once again the adults in her life were making major decisions about her well-being regardless of how she felt about it. Her grandmother called her to the kitchen table. "April, have a seat. We need to talk."

Whenever her grandmother said, "We need to talk", it was never a good thing. So she sat down in the chair furthest away from her elder and braced herself. "You know that your mom is ready for all of you to go back home."

April rolled her eyes and thought *here we go again.* "And go where? To her new apartment? It's not big enough for the four of us to live in."

"Well that's where Pastor and I come in. Since my house is still on the market, Zachariah thought that I should rent it out. So I'm going to let my daughter and grandkids move back in."

April could tell by the goofy grin on her face that she was expecting her to be excited. Moving back into her grandmother's old house was more familiar to her than her mother's apartment. But truthfully, the house was almost as small as an apartment.

Her grandmother threw up her hands and her chest jiggled. "Don't you have anything to say? I thought that you would be happy about moving back so you would be closer to some of your friends."

April couldn't help the grin that spread across her face. "I am happy about that." Her smile disappeared as quickly as it appeared. "But your house is small Grandma. I'm going to be back in a room with Brooklyn again if we move back there."

Her grandmother reached across the table and grabbed her hands. "That's what I wanted to talk to you about. After all these years I am going to have the basement finished. That means it will get heat in the winter and air in the summer. Zachariah knows a contractor who is going to put new carpet and padding down and put up insulation and walls so there will be two bedrooms down there. So everyone will have their own room."

"Really?" Maybe this wasn't going to be so bad

after all. April needed to ask one more question to be sure. "What school will I be going to?"

"That's the best part, baby. Everyone gets to stay at Grove Wood Academy." April sighed so her grandmother continued. "I know that you were looking forward to going to high school with your friends, but you are getting a better education right where you are. You can see your old friends in the neighborhood. That way you can have the best of both worlds."

April twisted her mouth. There were a lot of differences between the schools she used to go to and the one she went to now. For instance, her school was always bragging about their low teacher-to-student ratio. The buildings themselves were newer and in much better condition. Since she repeated the eighth grade, she went on the tour of the high school two years in a row. So she knew that her current school was better, but it wasn't like she wanted to be a doctor or lawyer like some of the kids she went to school with. In fact, she didn't know what she wanted to do when she graduated. The only thing she cared about was singing. Maybe she would try to have a career doing what she loved. She didn't need to get good grades in Biology or Algebra to do that. So why couldn't she go to the school she really wanted to go to? But it was pointless arguing. April knew that the decisions had already been made. She gently wiggled her hands loose from her grandmother's grip.

They remained quiet for a couple minutes until her grandmother broke the silence. "So I wanted to speak to you by yourself, because I know that you are having a harder time forgiving your mother than your brother and sister."

Interrupting her grandmother, April spoke up, "You didn't want to forgive her either. So what changed your mind?"

April noticed that her grandmother paused for a minute like she was trying to figure out exactly what to say. She sat back in her chair and began, "Honestly, I don't really have a choice. Felicia is my daughter and I love her. I had to remind myself that she was a good mother before she started using drugs and pray that she can be a good mother again. But we are never going to find out if she can do it if we don't give her a second chance."

"Second chance? Huh. More like the fifth chance," April spewed out her reaction and folded her arms.

"The truth is that if we want God to forgive us, we have to learn to forgive each other."

April was staring at her like she was crazy. She was trying not to be disrespectful, but she really didn't feel like hearing passages from the Bible right now.

"Okay let me put it to you this way. The court never took you away from your mother. She called me for help when she got arrested and I gave it to her. She is clean, so if we go to court she would probably win anyway. And she would be so angry with me that she might keep me away from you kids like she did before. Remember that?"

April unfolded her arms and sighed. "Yes ma'am, I remember."

"I don't want that to happen again. Do you?"

April shook her head.

"So it's better that I work with her than against her. This way you will be back at my old house and you can drive yourself over here whenever you like."

Smiling, April asked, "So that means I get to take my car with me?"

"Of course it does. It's yours. And if you don't spend the night over here Saturday night, you can set your alarm and drive yourself to Mt. Zion Sunday morning to sing in the choir."

April enthusiastically added, "I can keep driving us back and forth to school. And I can drive myself to choir rehearsal in the middle of the week."

Both of them exchanged smiles about that. Then her grandmother turned serious again. "I'm still going to be here for you baby. No matter what your mother tells you, don't you ever keep it a secret if she gets into trouble again." She closed her eyes and shook her head. "When I think about the way all of you were living before I came and rescued you it breaks my heart. And I will never let you live like that again." Her smile returned. "But I really think your mother is better now. What do you think?"

April shrugged. "I think she is better too. I just hope

she stays that way." She exhaled and looked her grandmother directly in her eyes. "But don't worry, I'm older and smarter now. She knew that doing drugs was wrong and if you found out you would take us away from her. So she lied about you to us to keep us away from you."

Mary held up her finger for her to stop April. "Listen, your mother did some things wrong, but she did some things right too. She called me to come get you when she realized she wasn't getting out of jail. The three of you could have ended up in the foster care system. Rarely do kids get to stay together, so you would have been separated from each other and alone."

"Wow. I didn't think about that. Brooklyn and Anthony get on my nerves, but I wouldn't want either of them to live anywhere else."

Her grandmother stood up and said, "Me either."

April sensed that their conversation was over and rose to her feet too. She watched her grandmother walk into the kitchen and open the refrigerator and knew that it was time for them to cook together. This was one thing that she was definitely going to miss when she moved back home with her mother since she didn't really like to cook. She headed to the sink to wash her hands.

"You're going to miss me when I'm gone, Grandma."

"No I'm not because we are going to see each other all the time. In fact, when you move I think you should start coming over right after service so you can keep helping me cook Sunday dinner for the family."

April hugged her from behind and took the family pack of chicken breasts from her hands.

32

Zachariah convinced his lawyer Paul to ride to the courthouse with him instead of meeting him there like he did with his regular clients. He figured that his lawyer had received enough money over the years from Mt. Zion to get some special treatment now that he needed him personally. So Zachariah and Paul reclined in the back seat of his Benz while Chuck chauffeured them through the busy gridlocked streets of Atlanta on their way downtown.

Most people had a fear of public speaking. Since he was a minister, he was never afraid to stand in front of a crowd and talk. But today, he was standing before a judge in a courtroom and that scared him more than he cared to admit. So he wanted to discuss his DUI case with Paul one more time before his arraignment. Zachariah hoped that the judge would dismiss his trumped-up charges all together or at least reduce it to reckless driving. His lawyer mentioned that the court did that occasionally for first-time offenders when the police forgot to read you your Miranda rights, they had no valid reason to pull you over, or they improperly administered the Breathalyzer test. But he told him not to get his hopes up about that happening.

Zachariah was adamant that the officer had no reason to pull him over other than he was a Black man driving an expensive car. It was late at night, so there weren't any witnesses around to vouch for this case of harassment. In a neighborhood like Cascade, Zachariah was certain that he wouldn't have been stopped on a busy street during the daytime. But Paul had warned him several times that accusing the police of racial discrimination didn't go over well with most judges. In fact, they tended to use the system to come down harder on defendants who made those allegations against the department because they didn't want everyone else to try to use that as their defense.

All of this was going to cost him a lot of time, money, and embarrassment regardless of the outcome of the case. The officer had taken away his driver's license on the spot and never given it back. And although Zachariah had gotten used to being driven around town since Paul suggested that he hire someone, he still wanted his license back. It shouldn't have been taken from him in the first place. It was humiliating the day that a cashier asked him for his driver's license when he was trying to make a purchase with his debit card. Chuck had to step in and make the purchase for him. In addition to that, he was risking points being added to his driving record which would cause his car insurance to increase, not to mention hundreds of dollars' worth of court fees and the retainer that he paid to Paul.

The stress was causing Zachariah to get agitated. He could feel his heart beating faster through his suit and knew that his blood pressure was rising. Doctors had warned him about taking better care of himself and staying away from stressful situations. He didn't seem to be doing a good job at either though. And with everything going on in his life with this case, trouble at home with Mary, all the money he was spending on the kids, the last thing he needed was to end up in the hospital because he suffered another heart attack. So he closed his eyes, took some deep breaths, and tried to remember the breathing exercise that his physician taught him. But it was so long ago. *Counting. It has something to do with breathing and counting.* Although he was trying to relax, the fact that he couldn't remember a simple technique upset him even more. He tried to open his clenched fists, but his hands wouldn't cooperate.

"Pastor Williams, are you alright? Do we need to pull over and get you some help?"

The sound of concern in his attorney's voice made Zachariah open his eyes and snap out of it. "I'm fine. Just trying to keep from having another heart attack."

Paul looked at him like he didn't know what to say, but quickly recovered. "Listen, relax. Today is just your pretrial hearing. When we get in the courtroom let me do all the talking. Don't go in there with an attitude about the cops not having reason to pull you over."

"But they didn't," Zachariah interrupted.

"Let me worry about proving that. I need you to stay quiet and humble."

Zachariah's nose wrinkled. "Humble?"

"Yes, humble. You can't go in there throwing your weight around like you do at the church and everywhere else. That might work for some people, but it won't work for you in front of a magistrate. This is my arena; trust me, I know."

Zachariah was a little offended by what he heard. He was paying Paul a lot of money and it wasn't to insult him. The way he sat staring at his attorney must have made him want to clarify his comment.

"What I mean is, you are an influential pastor in one of the biggest Baptist churches in the city. You are used to people doing what you want to please you, most of the time without you having to ask. It's simply done for you." Paul started speaking with his hands. "But that's not the way it happens in court. No one is going to bend over backwards for you. I've seen you get upset and say some insensitive things when you don't get your way. Honestly, sometimes you come off as intimidating."

Before he knew it, Zachariah's fists were clenched tight again. "Intimidating?" He shook his head in disbelief. "I haven't been called that in twenty years."

"That's because everyone around you is too scared to say it."

"Well if that's true, then why aren't you afraid?"

"Because I want to win this case just as much as you do. Which is why I'm asking you to be quiet, stay humble, and let me do what you are paying me to do."

Zachariah rubbed his hands together, but didn't answer. Paul was correct. Zachariah wasn't used to being spoken to like this. But he had not thought about his situation from Paul's point of view. Defending a minister with drunk driving charges would be an important case for him. He was already a well-known lawyer, but would gain more fame if he won. Paul started talking again, interrupting his thoughts.

"We do have a chance to beat this thing. Like I said you are well respected in the community, this is your first offense, there wasn't any injury or damages caused, and you used mouthwash which could have interfered with the test results." Paul paused for a second. "That being said, it's your word against the officer's about being pulled over. So you can't lose your cool if they say something you don't like."

"I got it. I'm not an idiot, you know."

Later that afternoon, Zachariah paced back and forth in his office at the church. Court hadn't gone as well as he hoped it would. The arresting officer's report stated that he watched him driving erratically for half a mile before he drove through the stop sign without stopping. The backup officer agreed that Zachariah appeared intoxicated to him as well during the detainment as he was being tested because his speech was slurred. Zachariah was there that night and knew that what they said wasn't true so he pled not guilty like Paul advised him to. But in an open courtroom the cop's side of the incident even sounded authentic to him. The judge decided that there was enough evidence against him to proceed to trial by jury of his peers, which is why he was wearing a path in his office rug trudging back and forth. Court ended hours ago and he was still upset. These incompetent men were lying on him and messing with his life and his reputation and he felt helplessly dependent on his lawyer to stop them.

"Pastor, can I come in?"

Zachariah turned toward the door. He gave his new secretary Stacy strict instructions that he didn't want to be disturbed, yet here Donald was knocking on his office door. Regretting his decision to go to Mt. Zion instead of the restaurant, Zachariah reluctantly told his assistant pastor to come in.

"What happened in court today?" Donald inquired.

On that note Zachariah sighed heavily and plopped his large frame down in his chair. Everything that he had been trying to hold back suddenly hit him that he was in serious trouble. After a minute he began rambling as if he didn't hear the question that was asked of him. "Have you ever felt like your entire life was falling apart? Like you made a couple stupid mistakes and things spiraled totally out of control, but you don't know how to stop it." He ran his hand across his hair. "Everyone started dying and I didn't know what to do. People look to me for answers, but what happens when I don't know the answers anymore myself? I mean I said the things I was supposed to say, but I wasn't sure if I meant them. And then I went to have one drink. Who hasn't wanted a drink when they had a horrible day? I just wanted one little drink." He paused and exhaled. "But I liked the way it made me feel. No, I liked that it helped me not to feel anymore. Then one drink turned into two, which turned into three. A couple days later I wanted to experience the same numbness that I felt before. So I did it again."

Donald sat down in one of the chairs in front of the desk and waited for his boss to continue. "Now I'm waking up on the cold bathroom floor next to the toilet. Mary must have put a blanket on me, but I don't remember laying down or her coming in there." Not able to look at him face to face, Zachariah focused his gaze on a picture of the front of Mt. Zion from twenty years ago. "I'm sad to say that wasn't the first time I've thrown up from drinking too much or the first time I've woken up in a strange place." Once he started confessing, he didn't want to stop. "One time I fell asleep in Walter's basement. He said that I went to sleep right in the middle of telling him a story about my mom and that he tried to wake me for ten minutes before leaving me alone. Another time, I fell asleep a block away from my house on the side of the road. The car was still running but it was in park. The thing is that I don't even remember pulling over. Once I got home I realized that I must have rolled down my window to throw up because vomit was splattered all over my window and the side of my car. So at three o'clock in morning I was washing my Mercedes with a water bottle and old restaurant napkins from my glove compartment like I was covering up a hit and run, because I didn't want my wife to come outside in the morning and see what I had done."

Both men remained quiet for a few seconds. Donald was the one that broke the silence. "Pastor, I don't think you simply fell asleep. I think you are blacking out. Sometimes people drink so much that they pass out and don't remember things." Zachariah didn't want to listen to what he was hearing. It wasn't so much what Donald was saying, it was the way he was talking to him. He was talking to him like he was ten and needed to be spoken to gently and this aggravated Zachariah. "From what I've seen going on the last few months and what you are telling me now, I believe that you have a drinking problem and we need to get you some help Pastor."

"Blacking out? You think I need help? No. I'm not that bad." He got up and started pacing again. "I just drink a little too much and get sleepy. I'm not a young man anymore, you know. But if all of this bad stuff would stop happening in my life I wouldn't need to take my mind off of my problems."

There was that look again. The assistant pastor had the same speechless look on his face as his two sons did at his house the day he got out of jail. Zachariah was tired of people looking at him like that. It wasn't as bad as everyone was making it seem. And if Donald didn't stop talking to him like that, he was going to be out of a job soon.

Raising his voice considerably, Donald continued talking to him. "Did you hear what you just said Zachariah? You said that you needed to drink to take your mind off of your problems. You needed it. Not you wanted, but you needed. We need our Lord and Savior. We need love and support from our families. Of course food and water are must-haves. There are a number of things that we need in this world, but alcohol should never be one of them."

Suddenly feeling lightheaded, Zachariah collapsed in his desk chair out of fear that his legs would give way.

33

Today was going to be a good day. After waiting nearly a month, Mary's OB/GYN appointment was this afternoon. The goal was to have her annual exam and tell her doctor about all the menopausal symptoms she was having. Hopefully, her female physician would prescribe something effective so she could get some relief from hot flashes, night sweats, and trouble sleeping. When she casually mentioned to her husband that she was about to get dressed to go to the doctor today he retorted, "Good, maybe she can do something about your mood swings too."

Mary wanted to tell him exactly what he could do with his opinion this early in the morning. She wanted to set him straight and inform him that his reckless behavior was the reason why she was always in a bad mood when he was around. But today was Valentine's Day. It was her favorite holiday of the year. He had already put a damper on the new year by getting arrested. But he was not going to ruin her cheerful mood by picking a fight with her. She had a lovely evening planned for them to try and lighten the tension around the house. It was Friday and the kids were spending the entire weekend with their mother, so they would have the house to themselves for a change. She figured that he would be happy about that.

"Happy Valentine's Day." Mary handed him a big red gift bag with tissue paper spilled out over the top of the bag. "It's just a little something to take to work with you today. I've got big plans for us when you get home this evening." He slowly took the bag from her hand and placed it on their dresser on his way to the bathroom. "Aren't you going to open it?"

"I've got to use the bathroom. I'll open it in a minute." All Mary could do was stand there in shock and watch her husband's back as he walked away and closed the bathroom door without even saying, "thank you" or "Happy Valentine's Day" in return.

Mary busied herself while waiting for him to return. She whipped the top sheet and duvet into place from her side of the bed and then walked around to adjust his side. Next, she propped and fluffed all ten pillows against the headboard. When she heard the shower running, it was crystal clear that Zachariah wasn't in a hurry to open her present. She stared at the closed bathroom door for a few seconds before turning on her heels and stomping up the stairs to wake the kids for school.

Zachariah must have taken the fastest shower on record, because by the time Mary made it back downstairs and started fixing the kids a warm breakfast, he was headed out the garage door to his car. She curiously looked up and asked, "Baby aren't you going to say goodbye?"

He closed the six-foot distance between them and gave her a dry kiss on her forehead. "Have a good day." And a few seconds later, he was out the door and she heard the garage door open and close shortly after. Once the kids left for school, Mary headed back to the master bedroom and noticed that her husband didn't even bother to open his present. She quickly wiped away the tears that rolled down her face and headed for a quick shower herself.

Did he forget that it is Valentine's Day? In the warm shower she reasoned that he had been so preoccupied with his DUI case that he had forgotten. That's why he rushed out of the house so that he could buy her something nice to make up for it before their date this evening. Convincing herself that was true brought a relieved smile to her face as she lathered up under the hot water.

Later that afternoon, Mary was back at home after a productive doctor's appointment. Her OB/GYN told her that she was having normal symptoms of menopause, prescribed her some hormone replacements, and set up a follow-up appointment to make sure that her medicine was helping. Next, she grabbed a few things for tonight's celebration while she waited for the pharmacy to fill her prescription. Then Mary headed home to set up the atmosphere for tonight.

She started prepping dinner. One of her husband's favorite dishes was lasagna, so that's what she was going to lovingly prepare for them. Once it was in the oven for the next two hours, Mary pulled out a box filled with new scented candles and positioned them all around the dining room, living room, and the master bathtub. After dinner, she planned to draw a soothing hot bubble bath for two.

A trip to their dresser to retrieve a new piece of lingerie for her and red boxers for him that she had tucked away in one of her drawers, reminded her of Zachariah's unopened present. She dug through the bag and pulled out the biggest present which was a ten by twelve framed wedding picture of them for his office bookshelf at the church. As she admired their beautiful pose in their wedding attire she imagined how nice it would look on his shelf. She'd grown tired of looking at photos from the last thirty years of his life with his first wife. There was no way that she could continue to compete with a dead woman. If he told her, "My first wife used to," one more time she was going to lose her religion and curse him out.

Suddenly it hit her like your mother would if you cursed at her. Today was the second anniversary of his first wife's passing. In all Mary's excitement about this being their first Valentine's Day as husband and wife and trying to lighten the mood of the house, it had totally slipped her mind. No wonder her husband wasn't in a good mood this morning. She immediately put down their picture and ran to the phone and tried to call him on his private line at church. No answer. Then she dialed his cell phone. Again, no answer.

As she sat on the bed with her hand over her eyes, she wondered how she had blocked out the former first lady's memory so much that an important day like today wasn't on her radar. But it seemed like every month there was a day that triggered her husband and made him mourn her loss even more. There was her birthday, their wedding anniversary, the holidays, even Joshua and David's birthdays reminded him of his late wife because she gave birth to them. Today was the anniversary of her death. Next would probably be Mother's Day. The fact that he insisted on staying in their old neighborhood meant he drove past there every day. When they drove past it together, Mary noticed that he looked up the street like he was longing to see her. She was exhausted just thinking about going through this emotional rollercoaster with him every year for the rest of their lives.

Imagining Zachariah spending the day out in the cold at Gloria's gravesite or slumped over a drink at a sports bar instead of being at home with his current wife was going to drive her insane. Since he wasn't answering his phone, Mary filled up a tall glass of the sweet tea she made especially for her husband to try and relax. The chocolate covered strawberries that she purchased for them to feed each other in bed were calling her name. She had to resist them, because if she started eating them without him she wouldn't be able to stop.

At eight o'clock she called Zachariah for the tenth time. When he didn't answer she lit a few candles, warmed up her dinner and ate alone in front of the living room TV. She must have seen the Diahann Caroll and James Earl Jones movie *Claudine* more than a dozen times, but she cried for the first time at the end when the entire family jumped on the back of the paddy wagon when one of them got arrested. By ten she was listening to jazz, soaking in a bubble bath full of red rose petals alone feeding herself chocolate and crying. The new lingerie and red boxers were neatly folded and placed back in the dresser drawer. A two-piece flannel pajama set with matching wool socks would be the only thing keeping her warm tonight as she said a prayer for her husband and turned out the nightstand light at midnight.

34

Mary called her friend Brenda three times this week. She had come to the realization that there were many things in her life that weren't going the way she wanted them to, but they were definitely worth fighting for. On her list of things were her marriage to Zachariah, the future of her grandkids, and her twenty-year friendship with Brenda. This was her third attempt to talk on the phone. If this didn't work, Mary would soon be pounding on Brenda's apartment door. On the fourth ring, right before it went to voicemail, Brenda finally picked up the phone.

"Hello."

"Well hello stranger. How have you been?"

"I'm fine. You?" Brenda answered without a hint of enthusiasm in her voice.

Mary could tell that she wasn't going to make this easy on her. But if the conversation she had with First Lady Ward was accurate, she wasn't going to let a tinge of jealousy on Brenda's end destroy the bond they had built. "Honestly, I'm not doing so well. And I miss talking to my friend. So I figured that I would give you a call."

There was silence on the other end of the phone. Mary knew that she heard her. Brenda had Caller ID so she had to know that she called her three days in a row. She sincerely expressed to her that she missed her, but got no response. Didn't their friendship mean anything to Brenda?

After the awkward silence Mary heard. "You are the reason we don't talk anymore. You were always too busy planning the wedding of your dreams and moving into your big fancy new house to have any time for little old me."

"That was a very busy time in my life. But the wedding is over and we are settled into the house. If you ever bothered to come over like I asked you to, you would know that." Instantly, Mary regretted snapping at her friend. She wanted to make peace, not argue with her.

"What did I need to come see your house for? You told me play-by-play every time you went to the store and bought anything as small as a pot or pan, or as big as a new piece of furniture. I heard all about your three thousand nine hundred fifty square foot, five-bedroom, three-and-a-half-bath, two-car-garage home with its chef style kitchen, all stainless steel appliances, and marble countertops. The main level master bedroom has two walk-in closets, a bathroom with his and her sinks, and separate tub and shower. Been told about the fireplace and the formal dining room. I know all about the basement home movie theater, game room for the kids, and Zachariah's man cave. And how the kids have the entire three-bedroom top level of the house all to themselves. So what did I need to come see it for?"

Mary's eyes narrowed and her nostrils began to flare, listening to her so-called friend spew out facts about her beautiful new home like it was deplorable. "How about to support your lifelong friend during an important time in her life?" She found herself shouting again.

"I came to the wedding, didn't I?"

Taken aback Mary asked, "Why wouldn't you come to my wedding?"

"Because other than bragging about all the things you were buying for the day, you didn't even include me in it. You could have at least made me a hostess or something. I asked you a million times if you needed my help with the planning, but you couldn't be bothered."

"I had a wedding planner to help me. And you know we decided to only have the kids stand up with us otherwise you would have been the first person I asked to be my maid of honor. The usher board automatically assumed they would seat people since that's what they do. I didn't mean to hurt your feelings Brenda. I just wanted you to come and enjoy yourself." Mary took a deep breath and calmed down before she continued. "Why didn't you tell me that's how you felt?"

"I don't know. I figured if you needed me you would have said so. You didn't say so, I figured you had a new life and didn't want or need me around anymore."

"That's the stupidest thing I ever heard," Mary shouted. "You are one of my best friends. I'm going to always want you around. That's why I told you all the details of my big day, wanted you to come see my new house, and tried to celebrate your birthday with you by taking you to lunch. I want you to be happy for me and celebrate milestones in my life just like I'm happy and want to celebrate yours with you."

Mary could hear her friend exhale into the other end of the phone. She had said enough and was waiting for Brenda to respond. "I'm sorry. It just seemed like you changed. People are always talking about how money changes people. So when you were constantly talking about all the things you were buying with your new money, I guess I got a little jealous. I figured it would only be a matter of time before you were hanging out with other rich people who you had more in common with than me. When I came back from the bathroom at that hoity-toity restaurant and saw you talking to the first lady of another church, I felt out of place like you would be better off hanging out with someone like her and not me."

"Okay let me stop you right there. If someone paid

me a million dollars, I would never pick a snob like First Lady Ward over a good friend like you."

Mary could hear Brenda giggling on the other end of the phone before she responded. "Well that's good to know. I feel like such a fool now. You are right, I should have been more supportive of you and the great things you have going on in your life right now. But don't worry, I'm here for you from now on no matter what."

A sigh of relief escaped Mary's lips. Before she knew it, tears started welling up in her eyes. When she said, "Thank you," she didn't recognize her own shaky voice.

"Are you crying? What's wrong?"

"I did have some great things going on in my life. But lately everything has been falling apart. The kids are about to go back to live with their mother and Zachariah has a drinking problem."

"What? Oh my God. Why didn't you call me?"

"I have been calling you. You haven't been answering."

It was quiet on the other end of the phone again. "Are you at home?"

"Yes. Why?"

"Okay, I'm on my way over there right now."

"Wait a minute. You don't have to do that."

"Don't be silly. I owe you a visit, remember?"

Mary cleared her throat to try and pull herself together. "Hold on. Before we get off the phone I want to ask you one thing. You described my house to a T. Did I really sound like that when I was talking to you?"

"Woman, you sounded like a real estate agent telling me all the selling points every time you mentioned your house. If I had a quarter every time you mention your chef style kitchen or walk-in-closet, I'd be rich like you."

Mary went from tearing up to an all-out belly hurting laugh. It took her a minute to wipe her eyes and catch her breath. "Maybe I should be the one apologizing to you. I'm truly sorry. I wasn't trying to brag. This is the house of my dreams. I was just so excited I didn't know what to do with myself."

"It's okay. We were both wrong I guess. But we can finish talking about that when I get there. I'll see you in a little while."

35

An hour later, Mary peeked out her front window in time to see Brenda emerging from her old black Buick Riviera. Her friend's car had seen better days but she still loved it, so that's all that mattered. Brenda curiously looked around like she was trying to figure out if she was in the right place. Mary quickly moved to open the door and welcome her in. "You made it." They both shared big smiles and a long hug in the doorway.

"I'm sorry I've been acting so stupid," Brenda began as she pulled away from Mary.

"Please don't start that again. We're past that." Mary smiled at her friend's car parked across from her Jag. "I see you got your baby out of the shop."

Brenda looked over her shoulder and smiled. "I'm going to leave her right there at the shop if she acts up again. She is getting old and costing me too much money."

Mary giggled and stepped aside so Brenda could enter. "Wow. This is nice, Mary." She looked directly in Mary's eyes and said, "Take me on a tour. I want to start at the top and work my way down. Show me everything."

Mary raised an eyebrow thinking that her friend was only trying to be polite. "Are you sure?" Brenda's answer was to take her shoes off and start walking up the stairs to the kid's rooms without her. Mary quickly followed and showed her friend every square inch of the house as requested. At first, she was a little leery about showing every feature that she was proud of, but Brenda genuinely seemed fascinated with everything. Mary eased into full tour guide mode saving her favorite room of the house, the kitchen until the very end. Because it was a weekday, the kids were at school and Zachariah was at the church. So they had the entire house to themselves. Mary fixed them soup, salad, and sandwiches for lunch and they settled in at the dining room table for some long overdue girl talk.

"So catch me up on what's been going on. Did you say the kids are going back to Felicia? Where has she been all this time?"

Exhaling and nodding her head Mary began explaining how Felicia said she was too ashamed to call when she got arrested again. But she went on to say how she was clean and working. She had been spending time with the kids and everyone agreed that they needed to be with each other again, but Mary was going to miss seeing them every day after being their primary caregiver for so long.

"Well where does she work? And where are they going to live?" Brenda wanted to know. Mary closed her eyes and sighed before answering. "Oh that doesn't seem good," her friend stated.

"She works at a strip club."

Brenda's eyes got big. "Say what now? Felicia is stripping?"

"No. Thank God. She works there as a waitress."

Brenda let out a sigh of relief. "I know it's not the best job in the world, but at least she isn't taking her clothes off Mary."

"I know, but I just wanted so much more for my baby. I wanted her to go to college and then get married and have kids. Instead she has three kids, no husband, and no college degree. And she is a recovering drug addict working at a strip club."

Mary's head was down trying to hide the fact that she was crying again. But she felt Brenda rubbing her back. She hadn't even noticed her get up and move closer to her. "It's going to be alright. At least she is clean. Maybe that's the only job she could find. You and Zachariah know a lot of people. Do you think you can help her find a better job?"

Raising her head, Mary wipes her tears away. "I

guess we could try and see if she'll let us. I thought it was going to be hard getting her to let me fix up my old house so that they could have enough rooms to move back there. But she came around. Maybe she'll let us help her with a job too. I'm sure she didn't like explaining to Jr. where she works. No little boy wants his mama working in a place like that."

"Okay. I'll see what I can come up with to help her out too." Brenda paused before continuing. "Now, did I hear you say that Pastor has a drinking problem?"

Mary focused on her friend's face to keep herself from falling apart again. "At first, I started noticing little things like him being irritated whenever the kids were around. Then he started working late more often and being very defensive about it. A couple of his friends passed away and he started acting distant and staying out late at night. And after the last funeral, he was drinking and embarrassing me in front of a room full of people at the widow's house."

"What?"

"He was drinking Rum and Coke right under everyone's nose. I think they assumed that he was drinking a soda and being a little out of character because his friend died. But I saw him pour alcohol in his cup."

Mary had to excuse herself to get a box of Kleenex to continue. "I used to know all of Zachariah's friends, but now he has a new friend named Walter that I still haven't met. I'm pretty sure that he doesn't want me to meet him because he is his drinking buddy." After wiping her eyes again Mary continued, "He doesn't answer his phone anymore when I call him. And on top of all that foolishness, he actually fired me from the church."

Raising her voice Brenda exclaimed, "He fired you?"

"He said that it was because Mt. Zion needed a full time secretary and I have other first lady duties to attend to. I think it was because I questioned him about us driving separate cars when we were going to the same place. He claimed it was in case he needed to attend to an emergency with a member of the church or I had to leave for an emergency with the kids. But I noticed that he always had to stop somewhere on his way home and he came home smelling like alcohol and breath mints. Oh but here is the kicker, he got a DUI."

Brenda let out a heavy sigh. "I know. I saw both of you on TV. I'm so sorry, Mary. I put my hand on the phone to call you so many times, but I didn't know what to say. I thought that it had to be some kind of horrible mistake. I had no idea that this was really happening."

"I know. And he got up in the pulpit before the entire congregation and lied by saying that it was all a big mistake. I had to sit there and be supportive even though I knew that he was lying through his teeth to everyone to protect his image."

Mary felt a little comfort from her friend rubbing her back again. "Does anyone else know that he really is drinking besides you?"

"After I bailed him out of jail for the DUI, I told his sons and the assistant pastor the truth, that he has a drinking problem. Of course that made things even worse between the two of us after that."

"But did they believe you?"

Mary thought about it and answered, "I honestly don't know."

36

"Pastor, are you going to be at the church for a while longer?" Zachariah liked the way Paul didn't bother with small talk but got right to the point when he called him.

"Yes. I'll be here for at least another couple of hours. Why?"

"I'm going to be on that side of town and there is something that I want you to see right away."

Suddenly uneasy, Zachariah asked, "Can you tell me what this is about?"

"I'd rather show you if that's okay with you."

Zachariah paused. His lawyer wasn't really giving him much of a choice. So he responded, "I'll see you when you get here then." Although he usually didn't like it when people dropped by the church without making an appointment at least a day in advance, he would have been happier if Paul had surprised him instead of calling ahead. With a stack of work on his desk, Zachariah wouldn't be able to concentrate on any of it worrying over what his attorney wanted him to see. He assumed that it was related to his DUI case and not any church business since that was all they talked about these days.

Two hours later, Paul finally arrived and Zachariah attempted to not seem as anxious as he was. "Remember when we talked about getting a copy of your arrest video?" Before Zachariah had time to answer, Paul continued. "Well I finally have it. But I've got to tell you that it doesn't look good."

Zachariah countered, "Why? Doesn't it show everything that I told you happened? Those cops pulled me over and hassled me for no reason other than I was a Black man driving a fancy car and it was the middle of the night."

Without saying another word, Paul pulled his laptop out of his briefcase. It took him a couple anxious minutes to get it turned on, put in his password and a few clicks before they were watching the video of the arrest. The dash camera showed the officer following behind him for several blocks. Zachariah eagerly waited for the footage to prove him right despite the warning that his attorney had given him. Instead, his heart sank and he watched in shock as he witnessed himself swerving over the yellow line like he was a ten-year-old driver whose feet couldn't quite touch the brake. Then instead of stopping at the stop sign, he went right through it as if it were invisible. That's when the officer hit his red and blue flashing lights and siren.

The volume was as high as it could go, but the sound was very faint. "License and proof of insurance please."

The video showed him lifting himself up. Zachariah knew that it was because his wallet was in his back pocket. The young officer took what was handed to him and walked back to his car for a few minutes.

He didn't even realize that he was being followed that night. Since Zachariah didn't remember any of this, he was thanking God that at least he had sense enough to stop. The only thing he recalled was being angry about getting pulled over when he was so close to being home and climbing into his warm bed. That's what must have been on his mind as the cop was shining his flashlight in his face, making him get out of his Mercedes Benz, and trying to ask him questions. "Can you step out of the vehicle please?"

They both watched the video in silence as Zachariah raised his left arm to block the intruding light from the officer's flashlight. With the officer's other hand already gripping the top of his gun in his holster, the pastor realized that he could have been shot and killed in an instant if the officer had an itchy trigger finger. After a few seconds he slowly emerged from the car still attempting to shield his eyes from the light. Once he was out of the car, the officer finally lowered his flashlight.

"Sir, where are you on your way to?"

"I'm on my way home. My wife is waiting for me to get there, so I've got to go," he slurred and pointed in the direction of his house while barely being able to hold himself up.

"How much have you had to drink tonight, sir?"

"Just a couple drinks," Zachariah quickly answered, but raised his voice, apparently irritated by the officer. "Why did you pull me over man? Was I speeding or something?"

The clean-cut White officer glanced away for a split second. But his full attention was quickly back on the man in front of him. A few moments later a second older African American cop came into the frame. His appearance seemed to make Zachariah stand up taller and try to straight up his clothes.

"No sir. I pulled you over because you were swerving and then you ran a stop sign. I'm going to administer a few tests to determine if you are intoxicated."

Zachariah's eyebrows and nose squished together and he looked at the other officer to see if he was going to stop this foolishness, but he didn't. "Don't you know who I am?"

The second officer answered, "I sure do. But I can't help you. You'd better pray God can get you out of this mess."

The Caucasian officer doing all the talking seemed oblivious to what they were talking about. He went on explaining how he wanted him to hold his head perfectly still but wanted his eyes to follow his pen. Once again, he pulled out his blinding flashlight and shined it in Zachariah's eyes while he slowly moved the pen from side to side and up and down several times.

Next, the officer demonstrated how he wanted Zachariah to walk nine steps in a straight line touching the heel of his shoe to the front of his other shoe each time. The officer looked normal during his demonstration. But when Zachariah did it, he didn't touch the shoe in front of him and he had to keep lifting his arms for balance like a tightrope walker even though he was on the ground. He closed his eyes and shook his head at the fact that he couldn't even follow the simple directions. Instead of taking nine steps, he only took seven and nearly fell down spinning around too fast to turn and go back the other way.

When he finally got back to his starting position, the cop asked him to lift one of his feet six to eight inches off the ground and hold it until he told him to put it down. That didn't seem so difficult to Zachariah now, but the officer went on to instruct him to look at his foot the entire time and count out loud. "If at any time you have to put your foot back down, lift it back up and keep counting until I tell you to stop."

Zachariah watched as he swayed from side to side trying to hold his foot up. He put it down a couple times, but picked it right back up as instructed. The obvious problem was that he couldn't seem to remember the proper order of his numbers and kept skipping them.

Then came another part that Zachariah didn't recall ever happening. Once he put down his foot he must have realized that he was in serious trouble and tried to reason with them. "Listen officers, I'm an old man. I can't do all this stuff you are asking me to do. But it has nothing to do with me being drunk, because I'm not."

The officers looked at each other. The second officer suggested that he take a Breathalyzer test if he wanted to prove to them that he wasn't intoxicated so he did. A few minutes later, after breathing as hard as he could into the machine, his nightmare was getting even worse. "Sir, do me a favor and put your hands behind your back. You are under arrest for driving under the influence."

Zachariah folded his hands in front of him and looked at the men like they had lost their minds. "Do you know who the hell I am?"

"Sir, don't earn yourself another charge. Put your hands behind your back now." The officer took one step closer and Zachariah swiftly did as he was told and was handcuffed and shoved in the back of the squad car.

Paul stopped the footage and exhaled. "Like I said. It looks really bad. You were weaving and you ran the stop sign. So he did have probable cause to pull you over. Not to mention that you did admit to drinking. You never told me that you admitted to drinking. There is only one other thing that might work in your favor besides it being your first offense and you using mouthwash only minutes before the test. You didn't have on your glasses and the officer never asked if you had problems with your eyes. So we could show that you in fact do have issues with your eyes that could account for you failing the sobriety tests. It's a long shot, but we can try."

Zachariah hid his face behind his open hands for a moment. When he moved his hands he pleaded. "Paul, I can't lose my congregation because of this. I had no idea that I didn't stop at the sign and was driving that wildly. What would happen if I plead guilty?"

37

Zachariah sat in the passenger seat of his car for a few minutes before getting out. His wife had been nagging him to come here for a couple months. Whenever she brought it up, it led to a heated argument or he would leave the house to avoid hearing her mouth altogether. Donald preached to him about coming during their intense conversation after his recent pretrial court appearance. Despite his drinking to the point of throwing up, blacking out, and his DUI, Zachariah still didn't want to believe that he had a problem. It wasn't until he saw the videotape of his arrest that a terrifying fear of losing his church crept up on him. Only a few days before seeing the footage, he was adamant that he didn't need any help. But his confidence was a little shaken now and he wasn't so sure anymore.

So after watching the dashcam recording at Mt. Zion, Paul advised him that if he decided to go for a plea bargain, it would help his case that he was already seeking assistance without being ordered by the court. Zachariah begrudgingly decided to attend his first AA meeting. So here he was sitting in the parking lot contemplating if he would actually go inside or order Chuck to burn rubber out the parking lot.

They must have passed seven or eight meeting places that he recognized from the internet while en route to his destination. But Zachariah decided upon this white suburban high school across town, north of the perimeter in hopes that his name or face wouldn't be recognized. Who attended the meetings and what they discussed was supposed to be kept confidential, but he wasn't taking any chances. He promised Mary, Donald, and Paul that he would attend an AA meeting, but technically, he never agreed that he would participate. Zachariah still wasn't sure if this was all a big waste of time. A bunch of depressed losers sitting around whining about their problems to a group of strangers didn't have any appeal to him.

After checking his watch, he realized that the meeting was due to start in a few minutes. A group of three adults walked across the parking lot to the main entrance of the school. He slowly got out of his car, told his driver that he would be back soon, and followed the crowd. The gathering was scheduled for seven o'clock PM, long after all the extracurricular sports activities were done, so the parking lot was nearly bare. He assumed everyone there was here for the same purpose as him. The only female in the group looked over her shoulder and smiled at him as they entered the media center. One of the men held the wooden door open for him and said, "Welcome. Glad to have you."

Inside the library, folks were standing and speaking to each other in small groups. Zachariah noticed a table with coffee and cookies but decided against making himself too at home. He went and sat down in one of the empty chairs that were facing each other in a circle. The tall White man he assumed was the leader of the group stood up and called the meeting to order. Once everyone was seated, he reminded the participants that the only requirement for attending the meetings was the desire to stop drinking. Looking around, Zachariah noticed everyone nodding their heads. Right now his desire was to look good when he went back to court, not lose his church, and get his wife off his back.

Mary had even mentioned the "D" word a couple of times. As the marriage counselor for Mt. Zion's members, he knew that he was a good man compared to what other wives complained their husbands were doing. He wasn't cheating on her, using her as a punching bag because the outside world was treating him badly, and he brought all of the money he earned home. Hearing the horror that some of his male friends went through getting divorced from their wives, he knew that he didn't want to go down that road with Mary. His friends went from loving supportive couples who had been married for many years that seemed to have it all to arch enemies exposing each other's secrets and defaming each other's character over a house full of memories, items small enough to put in a safety deposit box, or someone's pension money. Zachariah had even seen one couple spend thousands of dollars in lawyer fees over a dog that they each loved but didn't want to give up. The lawyers were the ones that came out on top. And in the end, the men always agreed that it was cheaper to keep her.

He loved Mary dearly, but he built Mt. Zion through years of sacrifice with his first wife and kids and didn't want to fight over it with her. She didn't have any legal claim to it as far as he was concerned, but he had seen several bitter women try to destroy everything their husbands had built out of spite. And even though he didn't want a separation from Mary, it was extremely hurtful that after all they had been through as friends, she had threatened to leave him at the first sign of trouble in their marriage. He thought that they were stronger than that. But maybe he was wrong. Maybe they got married too soon.

Everyone in the meeting took turns standing and saying hello to the group. There were about fifteen people in the circle. The man directly next to him spoke up, "Hi. My name is Rick and I'm an alcoholic."

"Hi Rick," answered the group.

All eyes were on Zachariah. The leader of the group announced, "Hi. I know this is your first time here. Just know that we value anonymity. Everything that is said here, stays here. That being said, you can either introduce yourself or pass."

Zachariah cleared his throat and said, "I'll pass."

The participants continued until everyone had introduced themselves. Then the leader said, "I want to thank Rick for introducing us to the wonderful speaker we had last week." A few people clapped while others shouted their agreement about the great job the orator did. Once they calmed down he continued, "This week we are going to discuss step number eight in our twelve step program." He pulled out some papers that were folded up in his back pocket. "As you know with step eight we are to make a list of all persons we have harmed and become willing to make amends to them all."

Zachariah studied the crowd assembled around him, there were more men than women. They ranged in ages from the thirties to sixties. All of them looked willing and eager to share their stories. He checked his watch and noticed that only ten minutes had passed. Which meant he still had fifty minutes until this gathering ended and he was free to leave.

"At the top of my list are my ex-wife Sarah and my kids Micah and Brittney. I've been trying to make my amends with Sarah for destroying our marriage of twenty years. She got out of bed, came to pick me up, and drove me home more times than I care to admit when bartenders and friends refused to give me my car keys. After doing this for five years, one day she informed me that she wasn't coming to get me. She said that I got in that mess by myself and I can get out of it by myself. And when I got home the next day the locks were changed."

Zachariah turned away from the speaker. *He*

thought there's no way in the world I'd let anyone lock me out of my own house.

"Of course I was pissed off at her because I felt like she abandoned me. I didn't realize until AA that I abandoned her a long time ago. God bless her, she held on as long as she could, but she had to look out for our kids." He paused and sighed. "Lord knows I was doing a horrible job with them as well. They never saw me because I came home drunk while they were sleeping every night. If they did see me, I was busy arguing with their mother about being drunk. So it was better for them that I wasn't there then."

A couple people spoke words of encouragement to him like they had been there and done that. Once the facilitator of the meeting was finished talking, another member spoke about how she had stolen money and neglected her ailing mother when she needed her the most. But now her mother was living with her and she was trying to take good care of her in her last days on Earth while recovering.

Another male who looked to be the youngest one in the room told his story next. He explained how he started binge drinking and experimenting with drugs when he was in college. By the time he got expelled for constantly being on academic probation, he had fathered two children by different girls after having lots of unprotected sex. Both girls dropped out and applied for child support. He confessed that fathering illegitimate kids and getting kicked out of school still didn't make him want to stop drinking though. His mother let him move back home, but told him that he had to get a job since he wasn't in college anymore. After being fired from one job after another, being arrested for two DUIs, and told by his mother that he was going to have to get out if he didn't get some help, he went through a detox program and started attending meetings regularly. He thanked God and AA for helping him turn his life around. After ten years of living in his childhood bedroom and accomplishing nothing with his life, he was finally sober, had a good job, was paying child support regularly, and was about to move into his first apartment at thirty years old.

Zachariah realized that the people there weren't depressed losers like he thought they would be before arriving. Most of them seemed like decent people who made stupid mistakes and let their lives spin out of control. But Zachariah contended that he wasn't like them. He wasn't stealing from anyone, neglecting babies or elders, and Mary never had to get out of her warm bed and come rescue him. The only person he was hurting was himself.

After what seemed like hours, the meeting finally began to wind down. A small collection plate was passed around the circle to take up donations for expenses. Zachariah reached into his wallet and gladly put in a twenty-dollar bill hoping that it meant he could finally leave. Suddenly the leader began speaking directly to him again. "Brother, we meet here every week at the same time. I hope that you join us and share your story with us next time. In the meantime, feel free to study *The Alcoholics Anonymous Big Book* to learn more about how we can help each other."

Zachariah nodded, thanked him, and left it at that. The session ended with everyone except him reciting the serenity prayer. Most of them stayed around chatting. Zachariah went to the leader and asked him to sign his paper that Paul had printed out for him, saying that he attended the meeting. Then he quickly exited being careful not to walk too close to anyone else leaving. Although he made it perfectly obvious that he didn't want to be bothered inside, Rick seemed to be the persistent type. He stood and waited holding the door open for the slow moving newcomer. "Will you be joining us again next week?"

Feeling annoyed, Zachariah checked his watch again before he spoke. As politely as he could muster he replied, "I'm not sure yet. I guess we will find out next week." Confident that he had made his point, Zachariah's lips moved into a grin.

Rick smirked and patted him on the back as he exited the doorway. As Zachariah walked away, Rick said, "Hope to see you next week Pastor Williams." Zachariah stopped and swiftly turned around. But all he could do was watch the host close the door and walk back down the hallway. He ran his hand down his face and shook his head. On his walk to his car, he wondered if Rick was the only one or if the entire room was just being polite and knew who he was all along.

38

"Hi baby. You look really nice," Felicia commented about April's curly hair, royal blue shirt with sheer sleeves, black dress pants, and three-inch heels.

"Thanks. I wanted to wear jeans, but Grandma said that people get dressed up for opening night so I needed to put on some nice pants or a dress."

Her grandmother was in the kitchen trying to act like she wasn't paying any attention to them. But April knew that she would come around the corner soon now that her name was mentioned. Right on cue they heard, "That's right. You can't use my tickets going down there looking crazy."

April and her mother both smiled while Brooklyn and Anthony Jr. sat quietly watching the exchange. Their grandmother was so old fashioned. She was sure that plenty of other people would have on jeans and other casual clothes, but that's not the way Mary Lewis operated. April couldn't remember the last time she had seen her grandma in a pair of jeans.

"Mom, I wanna thank you again for giving us these tickets to the play. It will give us a chance to spend some much-needed alone time together."

April looked down at her shoes, slightly uncomfortable. With her new interest in theatre because of school, no one had to twist her arm to get her to go to a play. She wasn't sure how she felt about going to see it alone with her mother though. It felt like a setup.

"Don't mention it. I bought those Jomandi Productions tickets when the lineup for this season's shows was first announced several months ago. But I couldn't seem to find anyone to go with me tonight. No sense in the tickets going to waste."

"Where is Pastor? He didn't want to go?" her mom asked.

"He doesn't really like plays. A ticket would have been wasted on him." Her grandmother wiped her hands on her apron like she was uncomfortable now too. "Now y'all go on and have fun and don't worry about us."

Brooklyn and Anthony jumped up off the bottom step to give their mother a goodbye hug before they ran back upstairs to return to playing in their separate rooms. April and her mother set out on their drive into town as instructed. They pulled into the crowded parking lot and April immediately smiled when she noticed the huge sign over all of the glass windows to the lobby with the theatre company's logo on it. The lobby was crowded with theatre patrons milling about waiting to be let in the theatre.

The ride was quick, but quiet. Now that they were at their destination, April noticed that her mother was just as excited as she was to be there. As they walked across the parking lot she said, "It's been a long time since I've been to a production. Your grandmother used to take me to plays all the time when I was younger."

"Really?" This was the first time April realized that love for the theatre wasn't something that started in her family with her. "What did she take you to see?"

"We saw lots of plays like *A Raisin in the Sun*, *The Wiz*, and every year at Christmas time we saw *The Black Nativity*."

"Wow. I never knew that."

They walked inside the building and gave the ladies their tickets. April looked around and noticed the large poster board for the play they were waiting to see. The woman in the picture had strong facial features, a perfectly manicured big afro framing her face, and dangling peace earrings hanging from her lobes. The image made April long to sit in her seat and view the production. She looked up the piece early and found out that it was about a man trying to reconnect with his estranged daughter. That's what made her wonder if her grandmother gave up her ticket so that April had the opportunity to bond with her mother. April found it hard to believe that a woman who knew as many people as her grandmother did, couldn't find someone to take with her tonight. Still, April was happy to be here. And so far her mother had been good company.

After the play, April asked her mother if it would be alright if they stuck around to see if they could get a glimpse of the actors. Her mother agreed so they hung around. One by one, the actors appeared. The lead actress even took a picture with April in front of the theatre company's banner. She couldn't wait to tell Robin and inform her what just happened. Expecting to go straight home, April was surprised when her mother asked her where she wanted to go eat. After a few seconds she said, "I think there is a Ruby Tuesday's by Grandma's house."

"Okay. I love their ribs. Let's go."

At the restaurant, their waitress seated them in the back not far from the bar area. They were enjoying each other's company like they used to do before her mother got messed up with drugs. It felt just like old times. Although April had plenty of tough questions that she felt like her mother needed to answer for her, she also didn't want to ruin the good time that they were having. Her grandmother's words about there being a time and a place for everything popped in her head. So she would wait until another time to bring it up. As they were eating their ribs and shrimp dinners, out of the corner of her eye April saw

Pastor walk in and take a seat at the bar. She was in such shock that her shrimp almost fell out of her mouth.

Earlier in the week, April overheard her grandmother and him arguing. She accused him of drinking because he was slurring. He yelled back that she was wrong, he had stopped drinking like he told her he would. And here he was at a bar not far from their house. She wondered what lie he would come up with this time.

"Close your mouth. Wait. What are you looking at?" Her mother turned her head and immediately noticed who she was looking at. She turned back toward April with her hand covering her mouth. "Wow."

April sat up taller in her seat and kept staring in his direction. She had half a mind to march over there so that he definitely saw her too. Her mother peeked over her shoulder at him again.

The bartender placed a dark drink in front of him as they both shook their heads. "I'm sure Grandma bought those tickets for the two of them to go to the performance tonight. He has been acting funny ever since we moved into that house. Grandma told us about his DUI, but I knew something was going on long before she told us. I hear him when he comes home in the middle of the night, because all that noise wakes me up. And sometimes I hear them arguing because my bedroom is right over theirs. That's how I know that he lied to her about not drinking anymore. We should go over there on our way out."

Her mother sighed. "As much as I think he is a

hypocrite and don't like the way he is lying to my mama or acting funny towards my kids, this is their problem. I want to enjoy our night and get you home safely. If he says anything stupid to either one of us, I would end up back in jail. And my babies are about to return home, so that's the last thing I need."

April took one last glare over at Pastor, now laughing with the man next to him, before giving the shrimp on her plate her full attention. Although she disagreed with her mother's logic, she decided to obey her. Besides, shrimp was one of her favorite foods and she had messed around and let him make her food get cold. She stuck another piece of her dinner in her mouth and continued her conversation about her dream of being a professional singer and actress with her dinner companion.

Her mother was smiling the entire time showing her approval and giving her words of encouragement. This is the woman that she remembered growing up. Not the woman who sat at their table smoking cigarettes and drinking beer while trying to come up with a scheme to get more money for drugs after she had pawned everything worth any value in their apartment. Her appearance had even gone back to the way it used to be. She had a cute hairstyle and her nails had a pretty shade of fuchsia polish on them. April didn't think they looked as good as they used to when she got her hair done at the salon and got a fresh manicure every week, like her grandmother did now. But she figured that her mother was saving money by doing them herself so that she could have money for her family. April respected her for that.

39

Zachariah gave his driver the night off so that he could make a detour on his way home. Chuck looked as if he wanted to question him but thought better of it. Zachariah wanted to stop drinking considerably before he stopped for good. Stopping cold turkey wasn't the way that his mind or body wanted to do it. He figured hanging out twice a week for a couple hours was a lot better than what he had been doing. Walter was a cool guy, but he didn't want to end up coming to the restaurant every day because his house was empty like his.

Later on as Zachariah drove up the street, he could see their bedroom light from the side of the house. This wasn't his usual one or two o'clock in the morning entrance, but he was surprised to see that Mary was still awake. The bar didn't close until one o'clock so he could still be out if he wanted to be. He hoped that she would appreciate the fact that he was home before midnight and give him credit for that.

But no such luck. Mary was on him like a cat pouncing on a rat as soon as he stepped in the bedroom. From her seated position with her back propped up against two pillows she spouted out her accusation. "I was happy when you finally agreed to go to AA because I thought that meant you were willing to change. But I guess I was wrong, since you've been out drinking again."

Zachariah exhaled feeling the refreshing taste of the mint he had just finished, "Why do you assume that I've been out drinking? We haven't even talked today."

"That's how I know that you've been out drinking. Because I called you twice tonight and you didn't answer your phone."

Zachariah stopped himself from checking his phone to see if she really did call twice. Mary called him so frequently that he changed the default vibration to none at all so that he wouldn't have to be bothered with her constant nagging. Zachariah could only assume that she was telling the truth. "Well I'm home now. What did you want?" he asked, trying to avoid an argument.

Mary narrowed her eyes and folded her arms across her chest. "Don't try to change the subject. Are you trying to say that you weren't out drinking?"

Zachariah briefly thought about lying, but something about the way his wife was looking at him daring him to lie warned him not to. "No. I did stop at the restaurant to talk to Walter," he answered honestly.

Mary rolled her eyes. She seemed to loathe his friend even though they had never even met before. Walter, on the other hand, appeared eager to meet her. But bringing his wife to his hangout spot was totally out of the question as far as he was concerned. Zachariah sat down with his back facing his wife, pulled off his black leather loafers, and rubbed his feet hoping that would be the end of this conversation, but knowing Mary it wasn't. Overall, you couldn't find a sweeter woman. But when she had a firm conviction about something, his loveable wife transformed. Her opinion was that he had a problem with alcohol. As long as she believed that, he wouldn't have any peace until she thought otherwise.

"I thought Paul advised you to stop drinking altogether."

"I said that I met with Walter. I wasn't drinking."

"Lie number one," Mary shouted. "April and Felicia saw you out tonight drinking."

He wanted to turn around and deny it, but he knew that she was telling the truth again. Felicia had been spending more time with the kids lately. Mary even asked for the names of members in the church that did carpentry work so that she could have the basement of her old house fixed up. Her plan was to start doing work on the house so that the kids could move there with their mother soon. Zachariah was happy about that. But not happy that their outing meant that they spotted him on his.

"Imagine my surprise when they came back from a play I sent them to and they decided to go to dinner close by and April blurted out that she saw you tonight."

As he contemplated what to say next, he suddenly realized that he was sitting in front of the dresser mirror and Mary was intently staring at him through it. He exhaled, got up to move closer to Mary, and settled on the truth. "I just had one drink, baby. It was no big deal."

She quickly moved her leg out of his reach when he tried to touch her. "It is a big deal and I don't understand why you can't see that." Mary paused and then asked, "Where is Chuck? Did you drive yourself home?"

Reluctantly Zachariah answered, "Yes I did, but I'm not drunk." He jumped up with his hands outstretched at his sides. "Do I look drunk to you?"

Mary shook her head and her eyes teared up. "You just don't get it, do you? Zachariah, you are a minister who is not supposed to be hanging out in bars every other night drinking. We haven't even been married a year yet and we are already headed for divorce."

"Stop saying that," he shouted. "You are not leaving me. And the Bible doesn't say that Christians can't have anything to drink."

"I wouldn't be so confident about me not leaving if I were you," she said, rolling her eyes. To challenge him further she continued, "The Bible says that you shouldn't get drunk with wine, but be filled with the spirit and that drunkards won't inherit the kingdom of God." She was out from under the covers sitting on the side of the bed now.

Zachariah chuckled and started unbuttoning his dress shirt. "Mary, you don't want to get into a Bible verse battle with me. Do I need to remind you that I went to seminary school?"

"You know what, you can quote all the Bible verses you want. But right is right and wrong is wrong." She put her head down and her tears finally started falling. She was openly weeping when she looked up and whined, "I don't understand why you started going out drinking in the first place. You weren't like that before. What did I do wrong?"

He hated to see women cry, especially a woman in his family like his wife. If anyone else had been the one causing her pain, he would have been the first one to protect her from it. But he knew that he was the reason she was crying. Zachariah went to Mary and took hold of her by her upper arms to gently pull her up close to him. "Please stop crying, baby. You didn't do anything wrong. I think the deaths of my friends really shook me up more than I want to admit. I started thinking that I could be next and just wanted to have some fun. The fact that everyone was telling me that I was doing something wrong, only made it more exciting to me." He pulled her chin up to face his. "I'm sorry baby. I've been acting like such a fool.

Please forgive me."

Not wanting to make any more promises that he ended up not keeping, he quietly pledged to himself to stop drinking once and for all. Tonight's drinks were the last ones he would ever have. He wasn't ready to die and go to his heavenly home like his friends had, but that didn't mean he had to be down here doing reckless things to make him lose Mary or Mt. Zion.

They stood there for a while quietly enjoying holding each other. Even though it was the end of the day, he could still smell her Shalimar Perfume like she had just sprayed it on. He loved that scent on her. It had been weeks since they touched each other and he felt himself wanting to make love to his wife. He attempted to have sex with her a few other times when he came home from the bar, but she was always angry and turned him down. When his wife reached up to rub the side of his face, he closed his eyes and thanked God that he hadn't lost her. Then he leaned his head down and kissed her on the lips softly at first and then wildly like he was trying to make up for lost time. He moved her back toward their bed carefully so that she wouldn't fall walking backwards and laid her down. Normally, one of them would turn the light off, but it was like they mutually decided that they needed to see and feel each other tonight. And they did.

40

"What does The Bible say about drinking?"
Zachariah paused to study the faces of the first few pews of
his congregation. Mary, Anthony Jr., and Brooklyn had
their usual front row seats this morning. Like he did several
months ago, Zachariah asked his wife to attend both
Sunday services to be his support system. It was a huge
relief to him that Mary came willingly this time around.
The deacons inquisitively stared back at him from their
normal spots. Over the years they had his back and
maintained a united front with him. He hoped that they
would not deviate after today's sermon. The other familiar
faces peering back at him waited for him to answer his own

question.

"I'm not going to be up here long today." He pushed his readers closer to his eyes.

One of his members answered, "Take your time, Pastor."

"I'm sure that most of you know that Jesus' very first miracle was to turn water into wine at the wedding at Cana. I've preached about that before, right here at Mt. Zion. That's in John 2:7, if you want to check your bibles," he said lifting the good book up like it was his proof. Then he began pacing in his pulpit. "I've reminded myself of that many nights while I was doing what I shouldn't have been doing. I said to myself, Jesus only performed seven miracles. Surely God wouldn't have let his only begotten son waste one of them on alcohol if He truly didn't want us to partake of it. And wasn't it Jesus Christ who hung out with sinners?"

One of the church nurses placed a white terry cloth towel on the podium for him. He hadn't realized until that very moment how profusely he was sweating. As he went to grab the towel, a drop of perspiration rolled off the tip of his nose onto his neatly written notes. Zachariah slowly dabbed all around his face and nodded a thank you to the nurse that was already back in her seat against the wall.

"You know that everyone thought that Noah was crazy for building the ark." A big smile spread across his face. "Until it rained."

That's when the congregation started responding.

"Amen." Then he got a couple of, "That's right, Pastor."

"But what some of you don't know is that Noah was an alcoholic." A hush came over the church again. "You heard me right. After the flood, he planted a vineyard that produced wine, and he began drinking it. They would find him naked in a tent drunk." Zachariah started pacing again to keep from looking out into the sanctuary. "Well you might ask, Pastor, why would he start drinking after he successfully did what God told him to do?" He took a deep breath and exhaled. "I believe that Noah was traumatized. What would you do if the Lord told you He was going to let it rain for forty days and forty nights and kill every living creature that wasn't on your ark?" The more he paced, the louder he preached. "God asked him to do an important task. He gave Noah specific directions." Zachariah wore a wireless microphone so his hands were moving up and down as he spoke. "He told him what kind of wood to use, how many levels to build it, and what animals to bring on board with him. Do you know how many years people laughed at Noah and called him crazy while he was constructing that ark? Then when he was finally finished, God said, 'Now get your family and the animals on the ark and shut the door."

Zachariah swayed back and forth at the podium. "Imagine rocking back and forth on a boat full of two of every kind of the smelliest animals known to man surrounded by water for that many days. Knowing that everyone else who was begging to get on the ark once it started raining was now dead." The saints seemed uncomfortable. So their pastor spoke softer and stood motionless, "That was a heavy burden for the Lord to place on Noah's shoulders. It's no wonder he broke."

He wiped his forehead with the rag again and continued. "First Corinthians 6:9 says that wrongdoers, like drunkards, will not inherit the kingdom of God. Ephesians 5:15 tells us to be careful how we live. Do not get drunk on wine which leads to debauchery. And Luke 21:33 says be careful or your heart will be weighed down with drunkenness and the anxieties of life and it will close on you suddenly like a trap."

Zachariah began to shake his head. "Saints, I have a confession to make. I let the death of a few people that I was very close with and life's problems get to me. I messed up Mount Zion and I'm seeking your forgiveness."

He was quiet for a few seconds as the congregation shouted. "It's okay, Pastor." Another replied, "We still love you, Pastor Williams."

"You see, in Luke 5:31, Jesus tells us that it's not the healthy who need a doctor. It's the sick. And it's not the righteous who need to be called to repent. It's the sinners. That's why He spent so much time with sinners. So I think if God can use people like Noah, Jacob who was a liar, Rahab who was a prostitute, and Moses who had anxiety, then He can use a man like me, too." David started playing the piano in the background. "How can I preach to you about sin if I was without sin? But I want to assure you that I'm going to get through this troubling season of my life and come out on the other end stronger for it. And I would be remiss if I didn't take this opportunity to invite anyone else who feels like they haven't been careful enough in the way they have been living their life to meet me at the front of the altar. Have you been living a life of sin and debauchery? Maybe you feel like you have fallen into a trap and can't get out. Well I'm here to tell you that Jesus is the answer to every trap that life throws at you. But you have to take the first step and follow His word. The doors of the church are now open." He backed away from the podium as the choir began to softly sing behind him.

One by one, people began to sidestep their way out of their pews and walk down the aisle to the front of the church. The rest of the congregation began to clap for the brave souls on their journey to seek salvation.

Zachariah slowly walked down the stairs with his arm outstretched shouting, "Won't you come? It's not too late." A few more people obeyed and ran down the pathway. David began to pound the keys faster and the choir began to sing louder as their pastor shook hands with the believers that walked down the aisle to the front to be saved or to join Mount Zion as members.

Epilogue

Mary was still on a natural high after successfully pulling off her very first Woman's Day event as the first lady of Mt. Zion Baptist Church. And she was so grateful to Brenda for stepping up and helping her with the planning of the event. Even though she had her own church that she was a regular member of for the last ten years, Brenda had been attending service with Mary for the last couple of months. She wanted to feel the energy in the environment and wanted the women to start to recognize her face so that she wouldn't be a stranger to them on the day of the event. Deep down, Mary was hoping that she could sway her best friend to start attending regularly long after the event they were planning together was over. It felt good having a true friend by her side. Still getting used to being a pastor's wife, Mary was unsure of who was genuinely trying to be nice to her and who was suddenly interested in her because of her status. She and Brenda had their ups and downs but she knew that she could trust her.

Female doorkeepers passed out programs and special offering envelopes to the ladies as they entered the building. The women's usher board members escorted them to pews careful to fill in the front and middle sections of the church first, because they were filming the event. Aside from a few exceptions such as the audio-visual people, minister of music, and the musicians, Mary didn't want any men permitted in the sanctuary on women's day. She wanted the day to be very special and came up with the idea to ask all of the women attending to wear purple to represent being queens. Even though she was busy running around handling last minute details with her volunteers, Mary noticed how lovely and regal all the ladies looked in various shades of purples and lavenders. Some wore dresses while others wore nice pants and blouses. She was warned that people would show up in other colors to stand out from the crowd, but she was relieved that everyone there was being respectfully obedient. At least one piece of their outfits or accessories was purple. Mary had even found a purple hat to go with her embellished suit. She kept her other accessories black so she wouldn't go overboard. Brenda looked beautiful in her lavender dress.

Mary peeked in one of the side doors to do a quick scan of the audience. It was a beautiful thing to see all the different shades of melanin and purple. She was specifically looking for Felicia but spotted her maid Erica on the fifth row. They shared a smile and a wave. She was delighted that her friend actually showed up to worship with her. They grew closer every time she came to Mary's house. Unfortunately, their quick weekly prayer time had not changed Erica's husband's behavior yet, but she was attending church now so that was at least a start.

With the promise that April would get another solo today, Felicia swore that she would attend. Besides hearing that her daughter snuck in the back of the sanctuary to witness her getting married, this will be the first time in years that Felicia attended church service. She hoped that her daughter could put aside her feelings about church folks long enough to hear her eldest child sing. Other than singing along with the radio, this would be the first time Felicia heard April seriously sing. Rehearsing every week with David had improved her range and made her sing even better than she did before. Mary knew that Felicia would be impressed by her baby.

All of her guest speakers had been picked up from the hotel by the deacons and dropped off at the church early. Mary wanted to deliver nothing but the best today. So she hired an up-and-coming national singer with one song on the radio and the local's favorite gospel group to sing songs with the women's choir. She went to the music room to see their last-minute rehearsal. Immediately, she noticed that April was smiling ear to ear listening to one of the celebrities belt out her verse. A few days earlier, Mary made sure to play songs for April from the solo artist and the group so that her granddaughter was aware of the magnitude of who was coming to their church. But April already knew who their guests were. She was proud that she was able to have April be a part of what she hoped to be the first of many events that she hosted as first lady.

Later on, from her seat in the pulpit she observed Felicia walk in about fifteen minutes late wearing a short body-hugging purple dress. It wasn't the most appropriate attire for church, but Mary was overjoyed that she even showed up. She wasn't going to ruin this momentous occasion by chastising her grown daughter about her wardrobe. Felicia was there in time to hear April perform and her first event was a huge success, so that's all that mattered to her.

At home, there was no more talk from her about divorce, because things were looking up in her marriage as well. The day after apologizing for his inappropriate behavior for about six months, Zachariah finally stopped denying that he had a drinking problem. In an effort to show her that he was going to change his ways, her husband even confessed to all of his bad behavior. She suspected most of it, but there were a few things that blew her mind like him drinking in the car after the bar closed and him blacking out. Which only proved to her that his problem was bigger than she suspected and she was right to worry so much. When she heard from April that he was drinking at a restaurant only a few minutes from their house, she thought that was a one-time thing. Mary didn't know that he was a regular there. All of her lonely nights in bed, she envisioned him with a hat and sunglasses on at a hole in the wall bar where no one would ever recognize him. Hearing that he was careless enough to openly drink at a popular restaurant let her know that it was only because of the grace of God that he hadn't totally ruined his reputation.

But now he regularly attended AA meetings a couple times a week and swore that he had not had a drink in sixty days. Since he was answering all of her phone calls and didn't work late nearly as much as he used to, Mary believed him. And it felt good that she hadn't heard any references to his drinking buddy Walter lately. If his lifestyle consisted of drinking as much as her husband used to, he was one person she didn't care if she ever met.

Mary was also relieved about the outcome of Zachariah's DUI case when he pled guilty. The judge had them all sitting on the edge of their seats when he cleared his throat to speak at sentencing. "Pastor Williams, since you are a leader in your community and have a large congregation, I would expect more from you. This type of behavior isn't something that I would foresee from a man of the cloth. I realize that if I were to give you the maximum time of twelve months in jail that it would not only affect you and your family, but your entire congregation as well. So I'm choosing not to do that at this time. But sir, I would recommend that you never step foot in my courtroom again, because I will not be so lenient the next time if you do."

She had to restrain herself from jumping up and down in the courtroom when the judge only sentenced him to continue going to AA meetings for six months, doing fifty hours of community service, suspended his license for ninety days, and ordered him to pay a thousand dollars in fines. Zachariah wasn't happy about the money he had to spend paying for his lawyer and the increased car insurance, but he seemed happy that the worst of it was all behind them.

It turned out that Zachariah was upset with Mary about her behavior as well. One day he sat her down and laid out a stack of credit card bills from the last six months in front of her. He told her to take her time and look them over line by line. Thirty minutes later, Mary had to admit to her husband and herself that she didn't realize how much money she had spent since they had been married. She wasn't trying to go overboard, but truthfully she had never had access to this much money her entire life. The next day, Mary felt so bad that she spent all day returning clothes that still had price tags on them from her walk-in closet. The day after that, she went through the storage room in the basement and did the same thing with home decor items that she hadn't put out yet. More importantly, she promised herself not to do any more impulse buying.

Now that the kids were back home with Felicia they could finally enjoy being newlyweds in their empty nest. Mary really missed not seeing her grandbabies every day, but she knew that they needed their mother just as much as she needed them. She was grateful that her house was still on the market to be able to help her daughter raise them in it. Proving that once again God knows what He was doing even when we don't.

Brenda's suggestion about Mary and Zachariah knowing a lot of people who could probably help Felicia get out of the strip club and get a better job stayed on

Mary's mind. One day when Joshua was complaining about being short-staffed at work, it suddenly hit her that they had a restaurant owner right in the family. It took a lot of convincing on her part to persuade Joshua to even interview Felicia. Mary promised him that her daughter was clean and had changed her ways. She begged him to at least meet with her and give her a second chance. Even though Joshua was very busy running his business and didn't always make it to church on Sunday mornings, he was attending Bible study during the week. And he spent enough time in church over the years to know the importance of forgiveness. So after talking to Mary for twenty minutes he reluctantly agreed to have Felicia come to his business.

Felicia also put up a fuss about not wanting to work for him, because he would still have resentment towards her for trying to blackmail him when April accused him of molesting her. Mary assured her that Joshua had forgiven her and told her that like it or not, they were stepbrother and sister now. She reminded her how much she wanted to get out of the strip club and have a respectable job that her kids could be proud of her for. It wasn't easy, but Felicia begrudgingly agreed to take a chance and go to her stepbrother's restaurant for an interview the next day.

Mary wondered if she was wasting her time, but was ecstatic when Felicia called her. She explained, "Our conversation started out so awkward Ma, but took a turn for the better when I impressed him with how professional and courteous I could be with customers. Joshua offered me the job on the spot." Felicia even surprised her when she said

FATHER, CAN YOU HEAR ME?

that she sincerely apologized to him for any harm she caused him before she left. Mary realized that this was a big step forward for their two families having Felicia and Joshua working together.

Life was good again. Mary decided to have a big Sunday dinner at her house and invited both sides of the family. So here she was moving around her kitchen cooking enough fried chicken, collard greens, macaroni and cheese, corn bread, and sweet potato pie to feed an army. Zachariah even attempted to help her out in the kitchen at one point, but she shooed him away. So he took off his suit and made himself more comfortable in khakis and a Polo shirt, then had a seat on the couch.

One by one the family began to arrive. April, Jr., and Brooklyn were first in the door, followed closely behind by Felicia and her boyfriend Michael. Then David and his wife came in walking slowly behind their waddling toddler. As the family was playing with the baby and catching up with each other, Joshua finally knocked on the front door. He walked in apologizing for being late, but Mary told him that it wasn't a big deal.

A few minutes later, everyone was standing in a circle around the dining room table with their heads bowed holding hands. On the wall directly behind the table hung a smaller version of the oil painting of them that hung on the wall at church. The busy artist finally finished the piece Mary commissioned him to paint months ago.

She stopped admiring it and squeezed Zachariah's hand as he blessed the food and thanked God for his wonderful supportive family and Mt. Zion Baptist Church. Everyone squeezed hands and said a collective, "Amen."

ABOUT THE AUTHOR

Nicole Scott writes faith-based family dramas to entertain and inspire women. Her writing credits include interviewing celebrities for national magazines. She is an avid reader and a member of a book club for over twenty-five years. The Cleveland native resides in Atlanta where she is working on her third novel. You can keep up with Nicole on Instagram @thenicolescott, Facebook @authornicolescott, and sign up for updates at AuthorNicoleScott.com.